RUNNING OUT OF ROAD

A NOVEL

Jillian Godsil

WHITNEY MORGAN

RUNNING OUT OF ROAD
Second Edition

Cover art and Illustrations
made by the Publisher
with the assistance of Midjourney

Paperback - ISBN: 978-1-962668-15-6
eBook - ISBN: 978-1-962668-18-7

To my family and children and friends.

To my own late fantastic mother, who bears no resemblance whatsoever to Bella's mother.

And a special thank you to Bart, who is disguised as George in this book.

RUNNING OUT OF ROAD

Biography

PART ONE 1

Chapter One
Chapter Two
Chapter Three
Chapter Four
Chapter Five
Chapter Six
Chapter Seven
Chapter Eight
Chapter Nine
Chapter Ten
Chapter Eleven
Chapter Twelve
Chapter Thirteen
Chapter Fourteen
Chapter Fifteen
Chapter Sixteen
Chapter Seventeen
Chapter Eighteen
Chapter Nineteen
Chapter Twenty
Chapter Twenty-One
Chapter Twenty-Two
Chapter Twenty-Three
Chapter Twenty-Five
Chapter Twenty-Six
Chapter Twenty-Seven
Chapter Twenty-Eight

Chapter Twenty-Nine
Chapter Thirty
Chapter Thirty-One
Chapter Thirty-Two
Chapter Thirty-Three
Chapter Thirty-Four
Chapter Thirty-Five
Chapter Thirty-Six
Chapter Thirty-Seven
Chapter Thirty-Eight
Chapter Thirty-Nine
Chapter Forty
Chapter Forty-One
Chapter Forty-Two
Chapter Forty-Three (or possibly earlier) 1985
Chapter Forty-Four (or possibly earlier)
Chapter Forty-Five (or possibly earlier)
Chapter Forty-Six (or possibly earlier)
Chapter Forty-Seven (or possibly earlier)
Chapter Forty-Eight
Chapter Forty-Nine

PART TWO 167

Chapter One
Chapter Two
Chapter Three
Chapter Four
Chapter Five
Chapter Six
Chapter Seven
Chapter Eight
Chapter Nine
Chapter Ten
Chapter Eleven

Chapter Twelve
Chapter Thirteen
Chapter Fourteen
Chapter Fifteen
Chapter Sixteen
Chapter Seventeen
Chapter Eighteen
Chapter Nineteen
Chapter Twenty
Chapter Twenty-One
Chapter Twenty-Two
Chapter Twenty-Three

PART THREE   223

Chapter One
Chapter Two
Chapter Three
Chapter Four
Chapter Five
Chapter Six
Chapter Seven
Chapter Eight
Chapter Nine
Chapter Ten
Chapter Eleven
Chapter Twelve
Chapter Thirteen
Chapter Fourteen
Chapter Fifteen
A Thank You!
Shop at Story.

Biography

Jillian Godsil has been a writer since she was very little. She had no doubt as to this career in her first decade of life. On entering her teens, she was just as adamant but strangely found little time to actually write fiction, only a few scattered attempts echoing whatever book she happened to be reading at the time.

Into her twenties, she found university and then travel absorbed her time. She lived in London, Sydney, and Singapore before returning to Ireland with her first husband and first child.

For her thirties, it was all marriage and her children, two girls, which occupied her, as did a very demanding job and restoration of a period house in Wicklow, South Ireland.

It was as she approached her forties; she suddenly went 'Whao! Where are my novels?' and realised for all her talk, she hadn't actually started, let alone finished any novels. In her final year of her thirties, she sat down and wrote her first children's novel, The Bell Tower. After this breakthrough, it only took her another six years and a divorce to write Running out of Road.

Today, ten years after writing her first novel, Jillian has finally emerged from the global financial crash but not before changing the law, running in the 2014 European Parliament Elections and earning 11,500 votes.

Jillian is now an OG (original gangster) in the Web3 sector and regularly speaks on the world stage. She has two radio shows in Ireland and has written a number of other books, including a trilogy of erotica which was intended to save her house from the banks. It didn't, but it has proved a popular dinner party talking point. Today she is writing again—it's her passion.

PART ONE

Chapter One

My mother called me ugly. She looked into my sloe-shaped eyes and called them slits. She slapped me and shouted at me to leave her alone. Aged ten, I fled from her presence to cry continuously in my room, clutching my faceless rag doll for comfort.

"Ugly slit eyes," she screamed at me more than once.

Aged fifteen, I slapped her back. The shock was palpable. She pushed her hand to her reddened cheek.

"No child of mine," she began, but I had already walked from the room. She did not slap me again.

My husband calls me handsome. I remember thinking it was a word for a man, not a woman, and certainly not a girl. Barely nineteen, I had long since left my mother behind. While she was sober, she hated me. When drunk, she was pitiful. No longer a figure of terror, the ties were easily cut.

My husband is the owner of the pub where I work. He is much older and chain-smokes. I tell him to smoke up as I am only interested in his life insurance. His response is to grab a part of me: a leg, an arm, a breast, and squeeze.

"There's life in the old dog yet," he growls.

Sex with my husband is all squeezing. His large hands manhandle me. Sometimes it is very good. He might grab my buttocks and shape me into him. His kisses are hard and nicotine-laden. The hardness of his kiss travels down through his body, and when I am in the mood, it feels good and strong.

Three years married, and it works after a fashion. I work it because it pleases me, mostly.

My lover calls me beautiful. His doe eyes are soft and full of gentle love. His hands are light, trembling as they cover my body. He is only nineteen, and I am his first. His kisses are sweet and melodious. I do not love him, but I love his loving me.

I sometimes make people uncomfortable. I know I do. I don't flinch away from eye contact. I say what I think. I don't give a fuck if people don't like me. I am who I am. I do what I do. Fuck them if they can't handle that. My lover is my secret, though. The line between bravery and foolhardiness is very thin. My husband, Brent, does not suffer fools gladly. I am not scared of him, but I do not provoke him all the same. Let him smoke on!

I joined the protest at the old post office. Why not? It gives me an excuse to leave the pub and meet my lover, Liam. His father is the main ringleader in the protest. He is a very wealthy man, and he leers at me, unbeknownst to Liam.

Once, while half-cut in the pub, he felt my breast while passing.

I stopped and told him to "stop the fuck grabbing me".

He feigned an accidental fall to show that it was all a mistake, and I could tell he was fearful Brent would discover. That night in bed, Brent, while thrusting into me, gasped, "What did Tom do to you?"

I slowly shook my head from side to side. No answer would suffice. Brent, I could tell, was turned on by the incident. Arrogant old goat, my husband likes to think that every man is jealous of his wife. Likes to think that every woman wonders what it is that got him his young, sloe-eyed bride. If I told them it was my mother's fault, they might not believe me. And neither would I.

In a different, parallel universe, Liam and I might have been school chums. I wonder what that might have been like. To go to school, to sit exams, maybe even to go on to college. I could say that I played truant, but that implies I rebelled against authority. In fact, most days my mother kept me home. It didn't matter what the social workers said or did. If the pressure got too hot, we just moved. We didn't have possessions as such. Our meagre belongings would fit into a couple of plastic bin bags. She claimed I had asthma or was ill or was missing. Never her fault. Over time, I learnt to play along. I reached a point where going to school was plain pointless. I agreed with her on this one thing.

I met Liam at the demonstration today. Looking both ways, in constant terror of Brent, he greets me. Liam can never greet me in public without looking like a startled rabbit caught in the headlights. I am surprised that no one has twigged. We are bonking like rabbits! I like to wind him up. Today, I pat him on the bum as I say hello. He nearly leaps ten feet in the air.

"Bella," he gasps. "Don't."

I smile at Liam, and he smiles back; he is putty in my hands. But then my hands are pretty good with putty.

It is the most boring protest I have ever had the misfortune to attend. Where are the rotten tomatoes? The linked supporters. The chains that bind us together – lord. The chanted slogans and banners. Instead, we have fucking boring letch, Tom Durley wanking on about the history of the village. He has borrowed the local councillor's canvassing car and microphone. And so he stands up in the open car roof space, advertising

"Cormac Brennan, Your Caring Councillor".

Can he not see how stupid he looks? The concerned and caring villagers are all nodding. I am nodding off.

"Come on, Liam."

I squeeze his hand and walk purposefully back to the car park. There is a children's playground to the left, and behind that a patch of scrubland, flanked on three sides with trees. We make our way to the scrubland. Me, unconcerned and swinging my arms. Liam, fearful and scampering beside me like a dog. No one is watching us. They are all watching boring Tom Durley, who at this moment has his uses.

Out of view, I pull the quarter bottle of whiskey out of my jacket and open it. It tastes good. Hot on the back of the throat and fiery down my neck. I watch Liam, and he is waiting his turn. For all his shyness and timidity, he likes his booze. I think he is an incipient alcoholic. I do it for the pleasure, but I think he does it for the need. That, or just being with me, makes Liam nervous.

As he throws back his head to drink, I start to pull at his belt.

"Not yet," he yelps. But I am already reaching down his trousers. I know Liam likes me being assertive. He says he prefers romantic fires and hand-holding, but alfresco sex blows his mind. Today I blow him, and he comes in a very short time. I haven't even lost the taste of the whiskey. He kisses me after, which is kind of him, especially when he knows where my tongue has been!

We only just make it back in time to see the demolition begin. Without thinking, I cheer when the ball crashes into the old wall, and it crumples like paper. I am not sure why I cheered. I liked the old post office. Liam and I met there many times and even lit a fire once. It was not a good idea; the smoke drove us out. Mary Crogan looks at me in disdain.

"Have you changed sides?" she asks.

I laugh and move away. Fecking old busybody. She is married to the village school teacher and thinks her station is elevated. She is still staring at me as I bump into someone. I turn, and it is Mr. Celebrity Chef. He was in the pub last night and recognised me. He was funny last night and very drunk by closing. Funny and gently lecherous.

"Ah Bella," he coos all friendly bonhomie. He places his hands on my shoulders and pulls me towards him. Instead of the Dublin 4 air kiss on either cheek, he lands one bang on my smacker! How kind of him, and he surely didn't know where my mouth had been before!

Chapter Two

It's not a crime to hit a dog. I never owned one before. I've often kicked a minging stray if it comes too close. Let's just say I don't give off dog-friendly vibes. Dogs tend to leave me alone: men, too, before I developed breasts. And even after.

Brent gave me the puppy. He wanted to tie me down. Soften those edges a little. Make me dependent on another living creature, or perhaps I read too much into his actions. Perhaps he just wanted a pup. I was not impressed. I shouted and shifted a bit. Stormed out, if I remember correctly and took off for the rest of the day. My recollection is a little hazy. Hazy because I ended up with a bottle of whiskey sitting on Baileys Bridge.

It's actually an aqueduct. Built in the past. Made to last. Made for jumping off; at least that's what Marie Wilson did. Just after I moved to Ballybawn. She came here at dawn, and by the time the hue and cry had followed her wake, she lay quite dead at the base, splattered across the rocks to one side.

I'm not bothered by morbid thoughts. I don't dwell on others' misfortunes. I do, however, wonder at the practicalities of her fall. Did she stand up and step out like a sleepwalker? Or did she kneel down first in supplication and tumble forward? Or pitch herself headfirst? I look over the edge, and despite the height, the ground, the rocks, and the grassy floor are all disquietingly close. Not much room for reflection as she fell. Forget the life passing before her eyes; all she'd be able for was a quick

"Oh Fuck" and then, splat! At least it would be fast.

I don't know why I was so cross about the pup. He is a white, short-haired pointer cross. A brown patch covers one eye, with another pressed into the small of his back. His ears, floppy when down, lift like super dog when alert. His long tail is white and skinny with a tuft of hairs at the end. The non-patched eye is pink. His nose is also pink and spotted. As are his ears. His paws are massive and he doesn't walk, he bounces.

When I return, Brent is pissed off. I am just pissed.

"You bloody reprobate," he shouts. George, our new pup, has pissed all over the back lounge.

"We're all very suited," I shout back. "You're pissed, I'm pissed, and the dog is just plain pissing all over." I start to laugh. I laugh big belly laughs, while Brent looks at me.

"Piss off," he shouts and storms back to the bar. I piss myself laughing while George bounces, barks, and bounds 'round the lounge. But that's enough about piss. And pups. And human pulp.

Chapter Three

So that's what the celebrity fool was after. Publicity and friends. Clever move though. I have to admire his gumption. He's really riding on the prodigal son trip now. You've never known he was a son of Ballybawn. With all those posh vowels. And cufflinks. And the way he ties his scarf, Rupert bear-like, flung casually over one shoulder. And how does it manage to stay there for fuck's sake?

His restaurant, in Dublin, is one of those piss- posh places where the only thing colder than the frozen margaritas are the snotty bitches with their Kate Moss waistcoats and five-inch heels. I'd spent some time working in the kitchens in similar restaurants. The women order salads and avoid the bread, but they swill down the wine like there's no tomorrow. When they do order proper meals, they just push the food 'round their plates and send them back half, less than half, eaten. I should have had my pup then; he could have dined like a king.

Jeff, our newly resident celebrity chef-in-town, is in the pub at five o'clock.

"Bella, Bella, a very large pint of the black stuff please," he coos at me. I watch him from under my eyes; I've never really seen a man coo before. He isn't effeminate. He is definitely a full-blooded male. But still he coos. Strange.

"So, it's true then," I ask.

"Yes, yes, I'm coming home," he beams.

"You'll get bored."

"Don't believe so."

And he suddenly turns to look at me full on. "Do you want a job?"

"I have a job."

"No, a proper job, you could be my maitre'd."

I laugh. I laugh right in his face. "Fuck off," is the only reply worth saying.

But Jeff just smiled and took a deep drink of his pint.

"We'll see," he proffers, but this time his cooing is a little cool. A cooling rather than a cooing. Such a difference a letter can make. "You never wrote, so I married another." How many soldiers returned to married lovers, not theirs anymore, just because of a letter, or rather the lack of one?

Brent quizzes me after. I am sitting in the back lounge, the dog lying across my lap.

"Put the mutt on the ground," he snarls as he sits down beside me and pushes George down. "What was Jeff talking about?"

"He offered me a job."

"The fuck he did!"

"You're right." I turn back to the television.

Brent leans over and tries to kiss me; his hand travels with speed and authority to my left tit.

I push my face away and turn my body across. "No."

He still pulls me back, and I recognise his mood. "God, I want you, Bella," he whispers into my hair.

I close my eyes, but I cannot make it stop. I don't want it to happen. Don't want it. Don't. Want. It. Do want it. God, why do I want it? Fuck you, Brent. Fuck me. And he does.

Chapter Four

George is goddamn awful to walk on a lead. All bounce and pull; my arms are twice the length they started. I now have a choke collar, but it's not great either. I just end up choking the poor bastard, and he has to stop because he is nearly dead. Not good for the soul. So much for quality time with my pet. I bring George out for a walk and choke him every other step. Great.

Mind you, when I get to the forestry, then it is fun. George is now leadless and consequently headless, feckless, clueless. He runs a mile a minute. He hares off one way, then bounds back another. Each time, he careers towards me, almost knocking me over.

"George, you arsehole," I roar when he clatters into me.

But I am laughing, laughing, laughing. I love George when he runs, runs like the wind. I am laughing too because I am meeting Liam, and I have not seen him for at least six sex days. Or rather, like George, six sexless days. We are both in our 'lesses' now. But mine is about to be put right.

George bowls into me again. I feel the familiar curses rising in my throat, but, hey, give the dog a break, give the dog a bone, give the girl a bone. Liam had better have a bone on.

I am early. George actually, fucking, stops. Still. My God, my Dog. There's that letter-thing again. Just switch them around this time. From God to Dog. There's a joke there, but I can't remember. Something to do with a dyslexic, or was that the jerk that came to the toga party as a goat?

I light up. I don't often smoke, but I like to wind Brent up sometimes. Then sometimes, I want to light up when he's not there, and I worry, well, wonder, if I might keep on going. Of course, I smoke grass. I am just not keen on the whole nicotine ride. Fat cats feeding off stupid fuckers. I could get angry, but mostly I can't be bothered. Life's too short for whatever the fuck it's too short for. Natch. There is Liam. Thank the living fuck. He is smiling. Beaming.

"Hi, Liam." I watch as George bounds over, and Liam, caught unawares, is almost knocked over.

As he recovers, "Hey, pooch," he coos.

God, is that catching? What is happening to the men in this place?

Our sex is so hungry, I feel faint. No, I want to faint. I want to keep doing this. I am breathless. Liam is wiped. Beamed. Beamed out. This is a fusion of alfresco and connection. I really feel it this time. Not before. Before, I wanted him. Wanted him to want me. Wanted to watch him. Apart. Now I am in the moment. In the groove. In the feeling. God, this is weird. Is it because he cood? Fuck, no. But what is happening to me? This is just sex. But it's better.

George looks on, bemused. He tried earlier to get involved, but Liam, uncharacteristically, kicked him off, and he yelped away. Now, he watches from a safe distance. Does he know what we have done? What we were doing? Did we know what we were doing? I look at Liam.

"Let's go get a pint."

Brent is busy talking with customers when we get back. I put George in the lockup and enter by the back. Liam walks in the front door and orders a pint. He beams his order. Brent looks at him, his tossed hair and beaming smile.

"You look like you just got laid, son," he smirks. Liam is so full that he just grins. Brent grins back. There is grin fever sweeping the pub just as I enter from the back. I grin too.

Brent looks at my grin. Liam's grin. The fucking dog's grin if he were here, no doubt, and did the fucking math. Fuck me. Or rather, no, really don't.

He turns to Liam, who is still fucking grinning. Ear to bloody ear.

"Get the fuck out of my pub," he pitches low and earnest. "And don't ever return if you have breath in your body, or I'll tear you limb from limb. And if you touch her again, I'll cut you from your scrawny balls to your fucking lips." He stopped and just looked at Liam. Whose grin fades fast. And he leaves fast.

That was one fuck of a costly pint.

Chapter Five

Brent is cross, cross, cross. To be honest, I'm a bit pissed off myself, and no jokes about the dog, please. My cover is blown. Brent is not going to cool down, let alone coo down, for quite some time. I am just going to have to ride it out. Or rather, not ride it out if I want to be coarse. Me, coarse? Pretentious, Moi? Whom am I kidding? And that's pure Snoopy in Charlie Brown.

I am just full of graffiti. I'm the wall that stopped the wail. Write on me, why don't you? Piss against me. Lean against me. I'm in neon. I'm just the whipping boy. I'm the poster girl for my generation. We're Generation Y, thank you. Don't know what the fuck it means. Please attach a definition to me, to it, to life. Give me another label. Ugly, once but no more. Now I'm so damned attractive, I'm fucked! Or not.

Brent is not Generation Y. He's not Generation X. Fuck, he's so geriatric he's the generation game. Soon he'll be zzzzz. But right now, he is so angry, it's palpable. Visible. I see it in the air when I walk past him. There's a whole halo of anger around him; burning, burning bright, like a tiger in the night. That's not right, I know. But I can't help it.

I am surprised in some ways at Brent. I thought him more shallow. I thought him less in love with me. There's that less again. He's not less at all. He's more. More than angry. More than cross. More than that. He, to be fair, has never cooed and never will. What's more, or rather less, is that he didn't take me last night. That's how he stakes his claim, normally. Sex is his defining tool, his weapon, his marker. But he must be hurt because he didn't even come to bed. I expected to be marked, and this is worse.

All the same, I want to be with Liam. Something has changed there. I haven't a fucking clue. Why the fuck are both of them changing? I am the change child, and I hate it. All I want now is fucking domesticity – shit, that's a lie – but I don't want change. I want my rules—which are none—in a place that is static.

I pass Brent in the hallway, in the pub, in the street. All I get is venomous looks. I think if the penalty were not too high, he would kill me. If Liam comes back, he'd certainly kill him. Tom has not been in the pub since, for which small mercy, I am very relieved.

Jeff is back again. Renovations are continuing apace at his restaurant. At least that is what he says. Can't be bothered to use simple talk. Has to bunch up at least two or three fine-sounding words, pitch them into crap-long sentences, roll them all up a wordy carpet, and then unleash it on the unsuspecting public. Thump. Whack. Have your dose of words. How did you find them? Tasty, tasty, very, very tasty. Sometimes I laugh, but more often I feel like gagging. Talk like a normal idiot, please. I want to talk to him about that job. Things are not so cosy at home here as you can imagine. A bit of breathing space would be good.

When I pluck up the courage, he is all ears and eyes. My, how big your ears are, Mr. Jeff? And how big your eyes are, Mr. Jeff? And how big your teeth are, Mr. Jeff? He breathes across me, the waft of the pint dark and warming.

"I think," he says bitchily, "that your attitude would not make for a welcoming Maitre'd, or indeed any front of house role. But I can offer you a job in purchasing if you want?"

I do want and terms are agreed. He wants to seal the deal with a drink, but I think my attitude might be less than favourable. I toy with the idea of telling him to fuck right off, but I can't be bloody bothered. Let him get his kicks elsewhere. Mad men, bitchy men, and scared men. I can't be fagged with any of them. I am turning lesbian instead. I will be the only gay in the village. Yeah, right, fuck off!

Chapter Six

What is home? I never had one as a child. Fuck, I was hardly a child before I became an adult. I left whatever it was that could be called home long before those apron strings should have been cut. Mine were never even untied properly. The crunch point came when I was fifteen. I slapped my mother during one of her drunken rages, and it was all over. But my mother did not die, did not set the house on fire or even take up with an unsuitable man who beat me up. Oh no, her revenge was much sweeter than that.

She got sober, and she got God.

By the time I was sixteen, I was gone. Fuck me, but she had done all in her power to create a retard and then when she had me totally twisted up, she took a straight road to totally fuck up my head. Well, I wasn't, fucking, having that. No thank you. Fifteen years of chaos, of madness, of sheer lunacy, and then, "Count Your Blessings"—I don't think so.

She got sober and religion overnight, virtually. Once the blurry double vision of alcohol cleared, she suddenly saw how God-damn hot priests were. She didn't need to fornicate—the alcoholic years had fermented her libido—but boy could she adore. Adore, adoration, and adulation. It gave her a purpose and a drive and a mission and a will and a determination and an obsession. It also gave her a much bigger stick to beat me than ever before.

But I wasn't having any of it.

"Fuck You," I said and sailed off into the sunset.

God, the naivety of it all. I thought I could wander over to my friend's house and bunk down there, but Kim's mother was having none of me.

"It is not possible for you to stay here," she said through clenched teeth.

To this day I am not sure which reason she finally chose to reject me on. Possibly because she thought I was a bad influence on her daughter. Probably because her hairy-assed boyfriend had stopped scratching his balls long enough to suggest I was a hottie. Definitely because it was easier to say no. Scrawny bitch, all I wanted was a bed.

I spent the first night at the bus stop. The second in the bus station. By day three, I was hungry, and I turned a trick. It was easier than I thought, and I earned fifty euros. I have to confess the punter was known to me. Kim's ball scratching step dad. Disgusting? Of course. Profitable? Yes. He felt sorry for me and subsequently gave me a month's rent in a hostel.

Naturally he wasn't my first but he was my first commercial trick. He was coming out of the pub about nine o'clock on day three and saw me walking up the street. Little did he know that I had walked up and down that street about a dozen times, not necessarily looking for anything but with nowhere to go. Funny phrase that – streetwalker – boy I knew what it meant after five hours of walking. He asked how I was, and then we were going back into the pub again. Six vodka and Red Bulls later, it was payback time. Not that he asked—specifically—just that I felt grateful and he felt horny. It was the least I could do. Actually it was the least I could do. He listened. He did talk to my breasts, but he listened.

He was like the Dad I never knew, except for the sex of course. He visited me twice a week. Panted into my ear and pushed into my body. Then lectured me on what to do. After a month, I decided that sex with lectures didn't do it for me, and I fucked off.

Sayonara fucker. Get a life. Go fuck your girlfriend. Go lecture your daughter. And don't confuse the two.

So, home for me is a pretty moveable feast.

I answered the advert in the paper.

"Come at six," says a breathless voice. Brent is out front, and I slip out the back.

Ballybawn is a small village. Home to just 7,000 souls at the last census. But like all Irish villages, it is expanding, whether it likes it or not. The house is near the edge of the village and is in shit-awful repair. Jesus, I think. I'd better become a smoker fast so I can be rejected out of hand!

The door opens, and there stands Brigid. Owner of the breathless voice.

"I have a God," I say quickly fishing in my bag for a fag. Fuck, none when I need them.

"A what?" she questions, and I repeat myself, dyslexically correct this time.

Only I bluster and say "I have a fucking dog." And while she blinks at the curse, she smiles at the dog bit.

"Much safer I think," she says.

And so my new home is with Brigid. So too is George's; once I tell Brent and him. Him and Brent. Brent and him. Once.

Chapter Seven

Brent can go one of two ways. Actually, he can go full fucking fifty ways. I am so unsure of what he will do. Already he has missed the obvious, and I am on thin ice. I thought I knew him, through and through, but not it seems.

I return from Brigid's, and he is in the bar serving still. I go back and start to pack. I just don't want a confrontation, but I am bristling all the same. Try me, try me, my body says.

I am not surprised that I have so little. I just don't own much, full stop, period. I look around the bedroom. Empty of me, never full of me. Echoes of me, maybe.

Brent first found me, discovered me, singing karaoke. Badly. Fuck I sang like a whore. Which is what I was. Kindness paid my bills, bought me a drink, listened to me. Fuck that, sex paid my bills, etcetera, etcetera, etcetera. If it's good enough for the King and I, why not for me? Why wash dishes when sex could buy me dinner, get me drunk and pay for clean sheets—at the start. I washed dishes too when dirty dishes were easier to clean than dirty men. It depended on my mood and the man of course.

Brent came into the bar and at first, I thought him another dirty man—which he was—but he put out too. Sometimes there are contracts that work. Ours had a time clause on it, though I am not sure he knew it at the time. Actually, the clause was activated from the beginning without his knowing. God help him. He was fucked from the start and thought I could un-fuck him somehow.

Three weeks after we met, I was living in his flat in Dublin. Six weeks on I was helping him renovate his pub in Ballybawn. Six months on, we were married.

Mother was not invited. No scandal there then. Neither were his folks. But guess what, they were fucking dead. His parents, of old age. His sister, of a fall. Did I mention the aqueduct and poor splattered Marie Wilson? She died the week before we were married. I'd say it was a fucking coincidence except it was jolly close—ha! That's irony. Brent would not stop the wedding—registry office, so no big deal—except his sister fell the week before. It was still only the two of us in Dublin, but I have to admit I felt pretty shitty.

That night, in the Shelbourne Hotel no less, we had our honeymoon night. Don't get me wrong, we'd done it every way twenty times before, but not married. Did it feel different? I wasn't sure at first. I'm quite the little cynic. I was pushing the buttons, testing the water. Brent was spiked too.

Then as he came, he breathed her name. "Marie," he exhaled.

It was only an exhalation of air, but I heard it quite clearly. And so, she jumped. I saw her turn. She did not kneel. She stood tall and raised her hands. That was the supplication. Then she stepped out. To nothingness. To fresh air. To pain. To death.

The time clause was ticking. It was only a matter of time. And now, his time is up.

Chapter Eight

Brigid has to be the most laid back yet fucked-up woman I have ever had the misfortune to know, let alone share a house with. She floats throughout the house, surrounded by an aura of serenity, with crystals lighting her way. Does she fuck! The woman is a mad thing. Certifiable. The men in white coats are coming to take her away. Soon please!

Actually, I like the silly bitch. She drinks like a teetotal on speed. Like she doesn't know she's gonna crash and burn. Like it's always the first time. At first, I am surprised. We start drinking to celebrate my arrival. I went out and bought two bottles of red wine, a bottle of vodka and a six pack of Red Bull. To be honest, I thought the booze might last the week. It barely survived the night.

Brigid drinks while sitting in a very upright position. She drinks with serious intent and at speed. One bottle of wine and six vodkas later, she turns pale and lies down. On the floor as she is. That is fine. George lies on top of her, and I turn on the telly. Both seem happy, and I am too.

At one o'clock I go to bed.

At two o'clock Brigid wakes up and wants to start off again. At first, I am cross, but then I start to laugh.

"Your dog," she says. "Your dog is not very gentlemanlike."

She is standing over me, and spittle gently floats through the air. I can see she is cross.

"He tried to take advantage," she says indignantly.

No sign of a slur and I would think her sober, except that I left her comatose in the living room an hour before.

"Hey, what can I say? My dog's got taste."

Brigid looks shocked for a moment. Then she throws her head back and laughs. More spittle floating in the air and I decide to get up before I am wet through.

Back in the living room, the telly is on. Surprise, surprise it's a reality tv show.

"You watch this crap?" Brigid asks me in all seriousness, those eyebrows raised to the heavens.

"Only at two o'clock in the bleeding morning and when my drunken housemate has left the telly on." I shake my head. This woman is going to do my head in. "Bad for the soul," I am informed.   Brigid is about to turn off the telly, but suddenly the remote is a very complicated piece of equipment. She investigates it closely before putting it down gingerly on the table.

"Better safe than sorry," she intones. "Now, where is my drink?"

However, she only lasts for one more vodka and Red Bull before puking her guts up. George looks on admiringly. He tries to sample her ware, but I boot him into the kitchen. Simple George thinks those pies are for him, but not so fast, Mr. Pieman.

I push wan-faced Brigid onto the sofa in the living room with a glass of water and a towel. I look at the sick on the floor. I can ignore it, or I can deal with it. Or I can just chuck kitchen towels on it and leave it for Brigid to deal with in the morning. Of course, the last choice is the best.

Even drunk and very sick, Brigid sits upright. She must have a poker up her ass. I am ever so slightly pissed off. I don't mind her drinking all my booze. I don't mind her getting drunk. But I do fucking mind the sick. I mean, who wants to live in a sick-smelling house? And I am not mopping up. I didn't tick the fucking nursemaid slot on the tenant application form.

Judgement suspended. I'll wait till tomorrow. Fuck knows I've not got many options. I leave her in the living room and go to bed. Late-night television can be so exciting when you can hardly focus, and the room is spinning. Don't get me wrong. I've been there, like, forever. It's just the puke that gets me.

An interesting start.

Chapter Nine

"Keep on moving please. Don't stop. Don't hold up the traffic." I remember the accident. It was a dog. Trapped in the escalator. I didn't see anything, but I heard the howls. It chilled me to the bone. I held my too-hot cardboard cup of coffee and moved out of the way. The security guard was pushing people away, arms outstretched, while another security man placed temporary barriers around the top of the escalator.

When I looked back, I saw through a gap in the moving crowds the poor dog. His front leg must have been caught in the step. His shrieks were awful. I felt suddenly sick. I dropped the still hot, still full carton of coffee into the nearest bin and left the station.

Walking swiftly away, I felt breathless. I was not sure why it upset me so. The intensity of the shrieks. The pain he must have felt. Just the awful inevitability of his demise. Maybe he reminded me of me. Stuck pig, stuck dog, stuck girl.

An hour earlier, I had met Mother's priest. Father Brennan. He was white-haired and loomed above me. His body seemed to arch over me. Maybe, it was because of his height. Maybe, I hadn't yet graduated to very high heels, but his very height was intimidating. My childhood had not included priests, much. I met them in school but not at mass.

We didn't do mass: one of the few strictures of mother's that I actually agreed with.

Mother, demure with hair pinned back, was bobbing like a toffee apple at Halloween. Father this and Father that as she put the kettle on and re-arranged the debris in the sitting room.

I sat in the far corner. As tightly coiled as a spring. My legs were crossed and wrapped around each other. I was so anywhere else than here. My life in the past four months had changed utterly. From the familiar to the ridiculous. I could handle a drunk mother but not this creation.

I never had a sober mother before, but God how she disappointed me. All this nodding, sighing, and bobbing. Drunk mother was so much better than this. I suddenly had a Stepford mother, complete with bob. Fifteen was the wrong age to change, mother. I needed you before. I need my freedom now.

"Well Kathleen," he loomed over me again. "How is school?"

I didn't answer. I stood up. Moved to the right where he was not.

"I am going out," I said. And left.

I went back to the station. I did not know where else to go. The barriers were down, and the dog was gone. I asked several porters in the station, but none knew what had happened to the dog. He was gone before their shift. I checked out the top of the escalator, but I could see nothing—neither blood nor hairs. Not anything to say a dog had been trapped here and possibly put down.

It's like that film with Jane Fonda—They shoot horses, Don't they? Mother's favourite. Or so she cried four months prior (pre suddenly sobriety). We had lived that life. We had travelled that road. We struggled to come to terms.

Change may be the only constant, but for me it was shit. The new model T mother was not baking cookies. She was going for the jugular. Death by numbers. Number one: I may have been a less than perfect mother, but now I have God, so I am good. Number two: you may well have mewed, yelled, and cried obscenities for the last four years or so, but hey, I'm in charge now, so Fuck the Shut up (cursing, out of earshot of priests, is allowed apparently).

Number three: "you will account for your time. Number four: you will join me on my personal salvation trail."

"Fuck off mother."

Chapter Ten

The first time I met Brent's sister, she was very drunk. Or rather, she became very drunk by the end of the evening. She was a doctor and was the elder sibling, her choice of word not mine. He teased her about her age, about her spinsterhood—fuck yes he used that word. I cringed for her, but she just laughed. Light, tear-shaped notes, cut like glass. The sound was both musical and discordant. It was hard to listen to without wincing.

Brent and I were together for two months, and Marie knew this.

When we met, her first question was "How long do you know Brent?"

"Long enough," I answered at the same time as Brent said "two months".

She visibly relaxed and smiled at me for the first time. I thought about smiling back, but I wasn't in on her joke. I grimaced instead. It wasn't a good look.

My first impressions were not good. I am infallible when it comes to judging people. Not judging whether they are good people or not. Oh no, just judging if I would like to spend time in their company. I may well hang out with rotten bastards, but I know I'm going to enjoy their company. I am never wrong. And I did not like Marie Wilson at all.

Dinner was a fucking boring affair. Talk centred on her work. Then politics. Then property. Then people in common with Marie and her brother. She paused long enough to quiz Brent on the pub's renovations. Then back to fuck boring commonalty. Even their dead parents.

"What would they think," she tinkled her cut glass laugh.

"Their two beautiful children never married and no hope of grandchildren." Tinkle, fucking tinkle went that laugh. How, I wonder what they are. Up above the sky so high. Like a diamond in the sky. Just what was she fucking talking about?

So, I opted to drink heavily instead. If I could not understand the pompous bitch then I may as well get wasted. Waste of a night, wasted that night. I know which one I'd choose every time. I settled into some serious drinking and refilled my glass time and again without bothering with the siblings; her word not mine.

Of course, now that I no longer had any interest in the conversation, she became interested in me.

"Bella, my dear," she asked. "But you must have a career or job. How can you survive? How did you survive?"

I looked at her. Marie Wilson. Doctor Marie Wilson. Poison poured into my heart. A cold stream of ice-cold poison. I never had her parents. I was never a beautiful child. I was an ugly child. An ugly child that could hurt out as well as hurt in. And truth was often the most effective weapon. It could slice to the bone. Fillet the flesh from the bone. Open the wound. Incise the flesh. Come on, Dr. Wilson, I am talking your language here. Talk the talk, walk the walk. Cut to the point. Sever all ties. Separate truth from lies. Part with the truth. Part of the truth. Parting from the path. Parting is such sweet pleasure. Pain is pleasure.

"I'm a prostitute. I live by having sex with men. With condoms. Even when giving them blowjobs." I am serious, and I look her in the eye.

"But now, I'm going to live with Brent, and he is going to look after me," I smile.

Brent bristles. I don't know him very well. I am unsure if I have amused or abused him. But his bristle is a precursor to humour. He looks at me with disbelief.

"You never wore a condom with me, Bella," he says with undisguised pleasure.

I never wore a condom with Brent because I was all out. I spent my last funds on booze not condoms. I did not expect to be with anyone that night. And after, he held me, and it felt okay. So, why not? Lap of the gods and all that.

This touching moment between Brent and me is broken by Marie's snort. Yes, she fucking well did snort. I can hardly believe it. Tinkle, tinkle, snort? That can't be right, can it? Her nostrils flared too. Maybe that's where the snort came from. I watch fascinated to see or hear if anything else extraordinary is going to come out of her mouth. Her nose. Her anus perhaps? Tinkle, tinkle, snort, fart. Oh, I can hear it now. The other diners stop eating, shocked at such behaviour. Raise their napkins to their noses, delicately fanning the stench away. Oh my, oh my.

I wait for the killer moment. The killer comment. The final coup de grace. Marie splutters now. I can't believe it. This festival, this cacophony of noises. Shall I deliver it now? Or wait for more surprises. I am at the edge of my seat in anticipation. The adrenaline is coursing through my veins, fighting with the red wine for space.

Oh, what the hell, I'll have to go for it. Can't leave the poor bitch in suspense any longer. It can't possibly get any worse for her? Or can it? Just watch this space, Dr. Marie Wilson.

"Of course," I say. "If Brent plays his cards right, I will marry him and bear his children."

Naturally, I don't mean the second bit, but hey, it's a showstopper.

And I thought not using condoms could lead to unwanted pregnancies not unwanted marriages.

Chapter Eleven

Work. The pastime of the rich. Milestone of the poor.
Necessary evil. Means to an end. Love the work you do, and
you'll never work a day in your life. What a load of bollocks!

Brigid is a schoolteacher. Primary. Teaches the
infants. Mewing brats. But Brigid is a font of endless
patience. She listens to each lisped comment with serious
intent. Nods vigorously. Answers emphatically; The brats
adore her. They crowd her when she arrives. They collect
around her desk.   They trail like wisps of smoke in her
wake.

Brigid never raises her voice. An eyebrow might go
up. Or more likely she blinks. Once, twice and three times.
There's the danger sign and the infants push back in worry.
Stumble back to their seats. Cower silently to hear her rebuke
them in her quiet voice. Never has the two times table been
listened to with such intent.

Those little darlings. Mummy's treasure, every one of
them. Anxious parents, especially those overbearing mothers,
press Brigid for the news that their child is a prodigy.

"Of course," they say crap-cunningly, "I'm sure all the
other children are doing the same, but my child read the
entire works of William Shakespeare the other night. Do you
think this might be unusual or a sign of special talent?"

Brigid is serene. "All my children are exceptional." And refuses to be drawn on the individual. They pester her, those mummies. They crowd around her desk. Loiter in school passageways. Jump out of corridors to canvass her opinion "just in passing". When other parents approach, they divert the conversation quickly and clumsily into the generality of schooling. Or weather.

Brigid blinks at them all. It doesn't work as well on pressing mummies as it does on their moonstruck sprogs. The mummies are all desensitised. They wear makeup to drop off their kids to school for God's sake. That and jersey track pants. Doesn't quite fucking figure.

Brigid has learnt the art of sailing to her advantage. When blinks do not work, she billows out her sails like a festooned galleon and cuts through the grasping females with ease. I can almost hear the swoosh as she rolls first on one side and then the other. Parents scatter before her like tenpin bowls. It's a strike! Well done Brigid!

Travelling home, she picks up organic vegetables, fair trade coffee, freshly baked rolls and two bottles of organic wine.

"My God, Brigid," I exclaim. "You are Mother Earth and a welcome one at that!"

Brigid just looks at me sadly, but with a glint in her eye. "If I'm Mother Earth," she says, "then you are a Space Cadet."

"I may be a fucking Space Cadet," I counter. "But I have superhuman, nay alien talents. Space cadets are very good around the house—it all comes from growing up in outer space where scrubbing is a rare but much prized talent. And some houses need such talent."

It is not surprising that there are some awful things that need doing in the house. The shower. Ohmygod, the shower. If I am not going to be electrocuted through dripping water and the electricals, then I am going to be consumed by the gloop that lives on the tiles. Brigid does not believe in bleach or other harmful, earth-unfriendly chemicals. I swear by them. Let me rephrase that. I fucking swear by them.

Did I say I am a good scrubber? Good with a scrubber? That's me. Like with like. If there was one thing I learnt in the fifteen years that I spent with my mother was that the only way to have a clean place was to clean it myself. Some of the kips we stayed in were appalling. Let me also rephrase that. All of the fucking kips we stayed in were fucking shite.

I never travelled without my marigolds and a bottle of bleach. Call me perverse. Call me strange. Call me that woman off the telly. But just don't call me after hours! Nor to mop up puke. Sorry, but a girl has got to have standards.

Day two with Brigid, and those marigolds are out. Brigid went to work, and so did I. She had mopped up the living room, but the windows were still wide open. I turn my attention instead to the bathroom. Three hours later and the room is clean. I am waiting on Liam to come and fix the electrics.

But I am not sure if he will come. I call him my boyfriend, but he is still only my lover. And I am married. And Brent is furious. And Marie is dead. What a fucking mess. Just please God don't let me get fucking electrocuted before I figure it all out.

Chapter Twelve

"So you've left him then?"

Liam states the obvious, and I ignore him. I am stretched across his body, and I idly stoke his stomach. It's not ticklish anymore. Just after sex it becomes so sensitive. He cannot bear to have me touch him.   He laughs and cringes at the same time. "Stop," he pants. "Stop."

Eventually I do. It's like a cat playing with a mouse, no less serious but without the deadly end. Unless Brent catches us together of course. Liam is very worried. He is scared. He will not come to my new house, where I have a bed of my own and clean sheets. Even a clean, if ever so slightly dangerous shower.

"I will die clean," I threaten him, but still he will not come.

There is a thin line between a lover and a boyfriend. It comes down to rights and responsibilities. He does not feel he has the rights, and therefore he will not shoulder the responsibilities. He takes only that which he can command, like a conquering soldier. He takes, he uses, he cuts a swathe through the enemy. He is soldier, not farmer. His business is killing not growing, attacking not nurturing, ravaging not fostering, lusting not husbanding. He is lover, not boyfriend.

What turns a lover into a boyfriend? Fuck if I know.

The scales are tipped as I am tupped. That moment in the forestry. The sharp light pierced my skin. Seared my skin. Eviscerated my skin. Flayed my skin and left me bare and exposed like the peeling winter bark. The wound was open and love crept in. God help me.

And now, I don't even know it. I just want to stroke and stroke. The cat playing with her victim, but the victim grows and grows until it is the size of a house. This is disaster. I don't know it but I can smell the stench on the wind. The bodies; charred and dangling from the trees. The rotten fruit hang low and tumble to the touch.

We are on the bridge. It is peaceful and green on top. The river runs under and over. The channel up here is still and quiet. The water below is fast and dark. Not the same substance it seems.

Liam gets up and stretches. He pulls up his trousers. He pulls his shirt over his head. I lie back, breasts lolling in the moonlight. It is fucking freezing, but I am still hot. His cum spurts as I sit up. Phlat, phalt, phlat. He turns and looks at me, raises an eyebrow.

"Come back," I say, but he is putting on his shoes. His job is finished. He has grown big as a house. He is not to be stopped.

Chapter Thirteen

Fuck, fuck, fuck. The fucking shower is now dripping water instead of jets. The head is clean, but the power is fucked. Surge, surge then phizz and drip, drip, drip. My hair is wet. The shampoo barely rinsed. I am fucking frozen. I am so pissed it is definitely not funny. Of course, Brigid is gone to work already, and there is no one else to blame but the dog.

"George, you fucking idiot," I yell. "What did you do to the fucking shower!"

George jumps round the bedroom to where I have retreated, fucking shampoo still in my hair. He jumps and bounces and barks all at the same time. He jumps onto my bed where he is definitely not allowed. I lunge at him, and he jumps backwards barking. He jumps, twisting his body first one way, then the other. How he loves this game. But I catch him a crack with my brush on his haunch, and he flips off the other side, giving me a reproachful look as he now disappears under the bed, my bra in his mouth.

Thump, thump his tail goes under the bed. I am now so fuck-roaring mad, I crawl under the bed after him. He retreats backwards, barking. He is not scared, no, not my George. But then, he didn't fuck up the shower, and he has the memory of a five-year-old. Even if I kick three bells of shit out of him, he will still greet me with a wagging body in the evening. Loves the shit that pays him attention. Any attention. All attention. When all you have is one person to mind you, then you will stick with that person. At least until you reach fifteen. The magical age. For me anyway. Poor old George is stuck at the magical age of five and will always come back to me. God love him, he is stuck in a groove and he can never escape. But he better give me back my bra or he won't live past fucking breakfast.

It is my first day at work for Jeff. How prescient. I arrive late with sticky hair. I am wearing my bra, so I do thank the fuck. So too does George. A feint to the left and a judicious grab at his tail returned my property. Not without a little hair pulling, but we are all okay now. George emerged from under the bed once he had no more toys. I pulled his ears, a little roughly, but he knew we were made up.

If Jeff thinks my hair is sticky, he takes no notice. Of my timekeeping, or rather lack of it, he is less than happy.

"I expected you forty minutes ago," he begins, a frown puckering, but I cut him off with a kiss.

Bang smack on the smacker. "Sorry, Jeff," I whisper into his mouth. "Won't happen again."

When I pull back to the regulation twelve inches face space, his frown is gone, and he is still puckered. But the pucker has fallen from his forehead to his mouth. Good Boy Jeff!

A small victory for which I am thankful. The rest of the morning is given over to following first Jeff, then Tony, the sous chef, then Natalie, the restaurant manager, round the restaurant. Deliveries began much earlier and hence Jeff's disapproval. And now I am to check each blade of chive, button mushroom, head of rocket, blushing tomato, carrot top, mange tout, butter bean, parsley bunch, garlic clove, new potato, red onion, white onion, garlic onion. There is much pawing and squeezing of the vegetables. I wonder if this is good for them. Good for the customers. Did everyone wash their hands? Just how much prodding does an onion need for fucks sake? Then I realise, I have been given a bum's rush. New girl, let's impress her. Squeeze the veg. Toss the spuds in the air. See, what wonderful produce I bring. See what I bring.

I may not be a top fucking chef, but once I get over the quality shite performance, it is just a question of counting. Did we get two boxes of lettuce? Check. Did we get billed for two boxes? Check. Are we being billed for iceberg or rocket? Check. Did we order it in the fucking first place? Check.

It is just a question of checks and balances. Check the balance. Balance the cheques. Life is the sum of input in and output out. Crap in. Shite out. Actually, even quality in, can shite out. Before she jumped. A goodly time before she jumped, Marie told me I was shite. Actually, her exact words were:

"You are a piece of excrement. You have stuck to the bottom of my brother's shoe with the tenacity and stench of unwanted shit."

It was strong language from Marie, but she had single handedly downed the most of a bottle of gin. I remember laughing. For Marie to curse was quite something. She flinched every time I expleted. Expleted. Excreted. Flinch, flinch.

Still, she jumped. Turned and saluted the night and pitched forward. Or since she drank the guts of a bottle of gin that night too, did she just stumble? Checks and balances. She checked and then she unbalanced. Stumble, stumble, tumble. Oh fuck I am dead.

"You are a shit," she told me and I heard the slur. Knew the drink. Recognised the symptoms. Knew the drunk. She swayed slightly. A puff of wind would blow her over. Perhaps it did that night. Checks and balances.

Brent reached over and pulled her to him. He gestured to me to leave. I had no desire to stay, but as I left I turned my head. He held her against his body to support her. She leant in. His hand held her close. Close against her ass. I left. Checks and balances. On balance, I knew that hold.

I realise that I am enjoying the atmosphere in the restaurant. There is activity in the kitchen. Already Tony is making the breads for the evening. The puddings are being prepared. Sauces are made. Specials discussed. Menus written up.

The restaurant is not open for lunch so the wait staff don't turn up till three o'clock. Then the linen is laid out. Glasses polished. Silverware cleaned. Stations set up. The kitchen is getting faster now. It is relaxed, but there is a quickening. The quick and the dead. Jack be nimble. Jack be quick. Jack jump over the candlestick. Poor Marie just jumped. Not quick, just dead. Or is that quickly dead?

The restaurant is a living, breathing organism. As the darkness falls, the candles are lit. Pools of light. I am not needed now, but I don't want to go. It feels good here. I feel good here.

Jeff is winding up his act. He is like that irritating English chef—the one with the Brylcreem hair—but not as goofy. He is good. I watch him. He moves quickly without unnecessary haste. Nothing is wasted when he cooks. It is like watching an athlete. A footballer. He is balletic, but you sense his menace. He doesn't curse, but no one gets in his way. I can't believe this is the same man that cooed or that wears his scarf Rupert Bear style. He is a different animal in the kitchen. Different and interesting.

I am watched too. The watcher is watched. Natalie narrows her eyes and follows my gaze. She is Jeff's girlfriend. He sleeps in her bed. Probably fixes the electrics. Or pays a man to fix them. She is cool enough to me. Checking me out as I check the vegetables. Female? Check. Attractive? Check. Single? No or is it yes? No one asks me, and I don't tell.

Hey, I don't fucking know myself. Except that I am fucking quick, and I am not fucking dead.

Chapter Fourteen

After they took Marie away in the ambulance, Brent moved into the spare room. The pub was old fashioned, square and for all its antiquity, lacked character and even comfort. The landing was divided into four equal parts: three bedrooms and one bathroom. High ceilings and skinny windows, it was cold and unfriendly. The spare bedroom was across the back and overlooked the long narrow garden.

I heard him that night and for the next six nights keening in the room. After the pub was closed. After the people were gone. The civil wedding was planned for the week following, and I doubted it would happen. I didn't fucking care to be honest. There was enough drama to last the week as it was. And I was not sure that marriage was the answer.

I liked Brent. I liked his sex. I liked his provision for me. No one had ever looked after me before. And I didn't count my mother. Mother dearest. Mommy dearest. Fuck off dearest.

Brent was honest, to a point. But he believed he was honest. That belief was more important than the mere fact of honesty itself. The fact he was living a fucking lie was neither here nor there. Or rather it meant he was all over the shop, all over the pub, all over the place. He just didn't know it himself.

He was a provider. And for then that was good enough for me. What was my part of the bargain? I'm not quite sure and I didn't examine the contract that closely. It was without doubt an escape route for me. A safe path. Was I any different from those middle-class girls who marry insurance brokers or bank managers with nice fat salaries and fat derrieres to match? To be honest—there's that word again—I thought Brent was getting a good bargain. If half-mad, crazy as a loon, street kids are your thing! But I'm being hard on myself.

Yes, I was at the game. Yes, I was taking chances. Drinking, smoking grass, doing the odd line of coke. But, to flip that—and as long as you are not comparing me to a nice middle class girl—I was cool. Young, with legs that went on forever, mad, unpredictable and good fun to be with. Hey, you don't get too many of my type to the pound!

Really, I was the kind of girl you wanted to fuck. To boast about to your friends—and hope that not too many of them had been there before. To bring to places. I was guaranteed to look great and make a splash. I could just as easily cause a fight. Or throw food over the host. Or snog the spouse. Or kick the dog. Or put out a cigarette on the furniture. There were many ways I could entertain. And Brent was up there and able for the most of them.

Marie just didn't get me. Or perhaps she did. Maybe she saw the threat early on. Brent had broken the rules and walked outside the recommended path. He knew deviance when he saw it. And I had it in spades. And I didn't fucking care.

Poor Brent was going to hell right up there with me, but from the outside no one knew. He couldn't tell. Maybe he saw me as a chance to swap one deviation with another, more obvious, less obvious one.

I swung open wide my legs and he pitched in. Could not believe his luck. With me he was so far left of centre, he was safe. But if I were a safe haven for Brent, I was the wreckers' rocks for Marie. An end to her carefully cultivated patchwork of lies. More than forty years in the making and then poof! All gone. How she must have hated me.

It didn't matter that I knew. I didn't really give a fuck. It made my part of the bargain easier to make. Take one damaged package; okay on the outside but rotten to the core and match it with another; cracked on the outside and, hey cracked on the inside too, and the expectations are pretty low.

To last three years was a pretty good show.

But the week that Marie jumped and died was tough. I owed her nothing but did not wish her dead. Brent owed her lots, and he surely didn't want her dead. Or maybe that was the only way he could take the next step. Or the only way that she could take the next step, just one step, step over; over and out.

And so, I married without a rival. Without the third. Without the three in the bed, the little one said, roll over, roll over. And so they all rolled over, and Marie fell out. And she gave a little shout. Roll over, roll over. And so they all rolled over, and she fell out. And the little one said. Fuck off, you're dead!

Chapter Fifteen

Brigid is impressed with my job. We sat that night after my first day at work. We drink wine, but not heavily. I note that Brigid has different paces of drinking. Tonight it is reflective. Much looking and swirling of the wine, although it doesn't deserve it. I discovered she has a boyfriend. A mechanic whom she sees every Tuesday night and most Saturdays. He is a keen motorbiker and often competes at the weekend. She disapproves but not enough to complain, just enough to abstain from his events.

"So, you have left your husband for good?" she questions.

No, I've fucking left him for bad. In sickness and disease. Till Marie's death we do part. Okay, it's three years too late but hey, I needed the provision. All her estate came directly to Brent. He got a lot of dosh from Marie. Our life together was to be pretty cosy after that. Or should have been. But Brent never spent a fucking penny of her money. Like it was blood money or something. Well, yes it was but who gives a fuck about that. I fought on and off for the right to spend the motherload but got nowhere, nada, fuck all.

"Yes."

There is silence for bit. The telly is on. Some inane chat show, I am not sure which. Neither of us are watching it but it is easier than silence right now. We are too new to talk without background noise.

"You have a boyfriend?" The tone is gentle, non-evasive despite the bluntness of the question. The eyebrows are raised, but the look is friendly.

I shrug. "There is someone I have been seeing," I begin.

Her eyebrows raise themselves even higher in question. Delicately. I never knew such inquisitive eyebrows!

"I don't know for sure. Ever since I left Brent, Liam is not there. Not for me. Not for now."

Brigid digests this piece of information. She swirls the seven euro bottle of plonk in her glass.   She sniffs. She looks. She drinks. "Let's arrange a night out," she says.

Four missed calls, six texts and a very shirty conversation later, we are all standing in the crowded, dark, noisy bar in Pussy Galores nightclub. We have gone "up to town" rather than drink in one of the local haunts. Liam was adamant about that. So, here we all are. And we have been here for some time now.

Mick the mechanic is hilarious. He is an aging hippy. A biker. A bonker. A frigging nut. His hair is grey and long, tied up in a ponytail. He is shorter than Brigid by a good six inches, and Brigid is not tall at all. I am in my six-inch heels, and he is only up to my fucking naval. He stares adoring up at my tits. But it is a good look. Liam is unperturbed. Small men do not worry Liam. He is amused by Mick's bright and travelling eyes. He arranges that I sit next to Mick. Liam talks animatedly with Brigid, about what, I am not sure. I struggle to eavesdrop, but Mick is too loud and too talkative for me to hear.

Mick loves his bike. I hear all about his fucking bike. He even invites me to have a go on his bike. I don't fucking think so, Mick. I smile at him, and he mistakes my smile for acquiescence.

"No, Mick, I don't fucking think so," I am forced to say out loud.

Mick just laughs. Maybe he is used to being turned down by six-foot girls. I expect he doesn't get to talk to too many women my height. I try to draw Liam and Brigid into our conversation, but again, I cannot get their attention before Mick starts on again about bikes, racing this time.

No, Mick, just because your bike would look good between my legs, does not mean that I am going to mount it, you or anything resembling a bike tonight, I smile.

"Fuck," I said it out loud this time.

But do you know what, Mick just laughs again. Boy, he must not get out often. Or get out often with six-foot girls. I could tell him that he is a boring shite, and he would still laugh. Fuck, did I say that out loud too?

I am not sure at this point. The music is very loud. Mick is laughing his head off. He wipes his nose every time he comes back from the jax. I placed an order earlier and have siphoned up several lines by this time. Mick gestures not to say anything to Brigid. I indicate the same. We are both finding the bikes very funny at this stage. Mind you, I am so out of my head, I am spouting motorbike poetry.

Liam comes back into my orbit at this time. His face pulls close to me and his eyes look in. It's not my soul he is searching for, just my sobriety. If he wanted my soul, that would be easier. There it is, moving across the dance floor. It seems smaller than me, but then souls tend not to wear six-inch heels.   I watch my soul dance and move wordlessly to follow it. Liam pulls at my hand, but I tear it away. My soul and I are now on the dance floor. We move in sycophantic symmetry.

I am God I tell my soul. So, you are, she coos back at me. So, you are. Larger than God and more sexy. You are universe and all that is in it. You are soul. We are soul. Our words are too big for us now. For me now. I do not have to speak. I just am. I move. We move. We dance our dance, our rhythm.

Liam is on the dance floor now. He pulls my soul from my embrace. I look down, and Mick is my soul. That is not possible. Since when did Mick become my soul? Where is my soul? I am angry. Not with Mick but with Liam. Liam is white faced and furious.

"We are leaving, now," he hisses at me.

His anger spills over me. Pours over me. Like a libation. Suddenly I am quenched. Suddenly I am desire. Liam sees the change and is even angrier. He grabs me by the arm and moves me to the exit. The car is parked outside. He pushes me into the passenger seat and starts the engine.

I am now awake. I am now drenched. I am now ready for Liam. But he is driving, and he is furious. I paw at him, and he jerks away, pushes me away. I curl up under my coat and look at him. He drives and drives. He drives and drives. He says nothing.

He looks at me. I am huddled under my coat, but my skirt is above my knees. Pushed up and open. He looks at me. I look back. His eyes are dark.

The car stops. It is parked. It is quiet. He looks at me. I open the coat, and he falls on me, kisses me, tastes me, eats me, devours me. He is on me. He is part of me. We move together. We dance our dance. He is of me, in me, part of me. He is fucking me. Up.

Chapter Sixteen

My eyeballs are pickled in salt. I scream as I try to open them. Bars of steel fasten on my forehead, and I am crushed. The pain is awful. Awe full. Fuck full. Shit full. I am in pain. My forehead creases as I try to open my pickled eyes. But each attempt just scratches across my retina. Like a nail torn down a blackboard, the pain etches into me. Fuck.

I lie there. The alarm is flung onto the ground. The radio still murmuring, but even its muted sound offends my ears. Tears across my forehead. Hammers into my brain. I have the mother of all hangovers.

There is a jackhammer in my brain every time I move, even slightly. Then it gets louder and I understand it is outside my head. It is outside my room. It is the door, or rather Brigid hammering on the door.

"Ug," I say, rising up an inch before collapsing back on my bed. Brigid sallies in, full sails, galleon proud and bearing down on me. Even in my fug I can tell she is fuck furious.

"Did you take coke last night?" she says.

I consider the question very seriously. Inside my head, the question is sucked in through my ears and makes its way through the various channels formed in my brain; like spaghetti junction, all flyovers, flyunders, junctions, screaming traffic lights or is that screaming traffic at lights, red of course. The question is moving all the time. Yes officer, I am moving on. No trouble, no sir. Moving towards the central nervous system, the node, the hub, the essence; except the centre is all fucked up, coked out, pissed up and shaking. There ain't no answers available today, no laydee.

With nowhere to go, the question circles. Perambulates. Circulates. Circumnavigates. Reverberates. Retaliates and spits itself out undone and inside out.

"Was there coke last night?" I echo.

Brigid looks at me. She has been looking at me throughout my internal traffic report. She looks at me. Then turns on her heel and walks out. Oh fuck, what did I say?

Work is not much better. My limbs are creased in all the right places. Arms fold up, legs fold down. The body is in working order but limp like a rag doll. I am doing the fucking checks and balances but I have to sit down. Touch me and I tipple over. What's your tipple, sir? Oh, just the regular. Tip me and I tip over. But I have a fucking attitude. Fuck me and I'll fuck you. The suppliers don't mess with me, tippler or not. I may be sitting, but they cannot see the shake. I sign nothing today, just giant careless squiggles. Try and spot the quaver in that my Lord.

I have an endless supply of coffee at my elbow. I am such a cow no one dares question my caffeine intake. As if. And slowly the fug drops down. Drops fatness from my eyes. I straighten up. Shake off the fatness, the fug, the flakiness that I have felt since morning. It still is morning but only by the clock.

My brain is starting to spark again. Lights flashing and connections made. Snap, crackle, the electrics are back in action. Frankenstein awakes, and the body moves. I am a bad black and white horror movie. The familiar one where the wires and shiny steel head cap quivers when the lights are turned on, when the electricity courses through the body. Behold, the miracle, the body awakes. Or was it the line I shared with Tony in the men's bathroom? Gleaming granite surface, dulled lights, even in daylight. Whoa, there is no daylight in the men's toilet. Just the dusty lilies and pollen dropping slow. Dropping slow, dropping. And then the lights come on. Flash. Full on. But there is no daylight in the men's toilet, and the bulbs are dull.

Chapter Seventeen

Brent is still stalking me from a distance. We are not talking, but I know he is watching my every move. Liam is right to be worried, after a fashion. But, I am more worried. Brent does not let things go. Or rather, things do not leave Brent. It is only when he is ready that they go, into the dustbin, the recycling centre, the fuck-off-and-die pile, whatever.

I was not a trophy wife, fuck no. But I was a watchable wife. Other men liked what they saw; not as wife material, fuck no, they'd have to be Brent-mad to marry me; but they liked my excitement, my scent. The women; well it depended on two things. How much their men liked me and how much they fucking cared. To be honest, it didn't matter how much their men liked me as I tend not to touch other people's dinners. Married or not.

There is only one other pub in the village, and naturally I now drink there. It is nicer than Brent's pub. Modern and a bit soulless, but it serves good steaks in the evening. Some nights I sit there. At the bar, by myself. Liam will not be seen with me in public—in the village. Brigid doesn't really like Murphy's. She says it is too neon, too bright. She has a point. I am wearing a black jumper, and the lights have picked up on dust particles; shit, it looks as though I have dandruff. Just what a girl needs to feel good about herself.

I am frankly a bit pissed off. I have left Brent. But he won't acknowledge the fact. He won't talk about the separation. He calls it my break. He says it through clenched teeth. We have only spoken once since I packed my bag. I came back for my passport which was in the safe.

"Where are you going?"

"Nowhere."

"Why the passport then?"

"Just in fucking case I do decide to go somewhere other than this fuck-hole."

Brent ignored my answer and glared at me.

"Let's talk about this break," he began.

I cut across him. "It is not a break. I have left you. I no longer wish to be married to you. Period. Full fucking stop!"

Brent breathed. A full exhalation, and I was worried. I stepped backwards. Passport clutched in hand.

"I have left you, and I am leaving the house now," as I walked backwards, step by step. Brent closed the distance quickly. He put his hand on the door and pushed it shut.

"We need to talk about your break," he began again. Eye ball to eye ball I out-stared him.

"I'm outa here," I said and left.

Quickly. I heard his breathing again as I left. Long, drawn out and frankly dangerous. I did not turn back. I kept right on moving. Moving on down. Moving along. Move along there folks, nothing to be seen. Only the broken shards of a marriage. It was cracked from the beginning. Only a matter of time. Time gentlemen please. Time. Please.

So, I am pissed with Brent. I am not sure what I am meant to do. Do I need to ring a solicitor? Everyone says keep them out. Only the lawyers win in divorce. I think I may have an inherent objection to solicitors. I don't know any. I have only seen them on the telly. Do I qualify for free legal aid? I just can't be arsed to do anything at the moment. I drink my beer. That's a nice thing to do. I can do the beer-drinking stuff.

And what do I want from Brent? Not much. Not half his pub. Maybe a couple of thousand. What do I need money for? Holidays? Buying a house? A car? Upgrading my accommodation? Drinking money? The restaurant pays fuck all. The only saving grace is that I am fed at work. At least one square meal a day.

I drink my beer. I look into the glass. It is empty again. How did that happen? All this thinking is thirsty work. Noel the barman is very attentive. The new pint is ready before the old is dead.

But before I can raise the amber nectar to my lips—that Aussie ad is whirling round my brain now—a familiar voice holds me.

"Kathleen," she says. I, Bella, named by me and for me, turn to greet my mother. Holy Fuck!

Chapter Eighteen

The year I left my mother was interesting. Isn't that what a shrink would say? Actually, I think that's what she did say! Not that I had a shrink. The local social worker on one of her infrequent visits sat down with me. Mother was perched on the other sofa. Hands clasped demurely across her knees. Hair tied back in a tidy bun. Angelic smile etched in a rictus-slash across her face.

I faced the two of them. Fifteen years of anger coursing through my veins. I shivered with emotion; fear and anger in equal parts.

"It is interesting that you feel the need to steal," the social worker—Anne, I think her name was—said.

Mother put her head, birdlike, on one side. "Yes, Kathleen," she said. "Why do you feel the need to steal?"

I could not believe it. I had spent the past five years stealing on a daily basis. Stealing bread to eat, chocolate to savour, sweets to enjoy, clothes to wear, CDs to listen to. You name it, I'd filched it. From high street shops, from supermarkets, from corner shops. I even stole on buses and from people in crowded shops. Quick, the hand went in. And out it came with something nice for me. What the eye could not see, was fine by me. And by Mother.

Half the time, she lay in a stupor on the sofa. Chain smoking and drinking, drinking, drinking from a cut glass goblet. The cut glass goblet was like the magic purse of nursery rhymes. It never seemed to empty. It was never put away. From early morning until night, the drink stayed level in the goblet. Each time Mother raised it to her mouth, she drank. Then slowly the hand would go down again. Goblet to the mouth, to the floor. To the mouth, to the floor.

Could she really not remember? The anger coursed through my veins and tried to spew out my mouth like vomitous puke. Like the puke that lay across the bathroom floor the nights she moved from wine to vodka.

I heard them murmuring together after I ran from the room, clutching my mouth. I really was going to puke. I could feel wave after wave of bile rise across my stomach. I barely made it to the bathroom where I dry retched into the toilet.

When I came out, Anne was gone, and Mother was moving magazines around in the lounge. She looked up as I came in.

"That was an interesting chat I had with Anne," and she smiled at me. Still moving and rearranging the debris in the room. "We are going to get you some help. A counsellor of your own. We can do it during school term and during school hours."

I looked at Mother. "I am not fucking going to see any retard counsellor," I said very slowly and clearly. Mother tipped her head to one side again and regarded me pleasantly.

"I'll talk to Father Brennan," she said happily. "He'll know what to do."

If it were not too fantastical, I would have laughed. Here was my suddenly sober Mother murmuring with social workers and priests. You don't get to murmur unless you were on very good terms. Had to be close to murmur. Within the circle. Within the clan. Within the gang. Within the Klux. Well, I wasn't having anything to do with this. I left the room and packed my bag.

Mother did not notice as she was preparing to go out to Mass. She applied her lipstick and slapped her lips together noisily. The red slash only highlighted her veiny cheeks. She peered closely at her reflection, twisting her mouth this way and that; a little moue of disapproval perhaps? The lipstick was sticky. When she parted her lips, it stuck moistly for a moment before opening with a sickening slide across her mouth. A drizzle thread of red quivered for a moment before snapping; back to her upper lip. She touched it with her little finger and wiped it away.

I went past her in the hall, my rucksack on my back. Yoo dell Eee, Yoo dell Eee, with a rucksack on my back. That was the last I saw of Mother.

Chapter Nineteen

I do not like thee, Mother. I like thee not. Why fastens thou upon my life and chews upon my misery. Drawn to the stench of failure, thou hastens quickly to my side, to snuff my scent, to rake my wounds, to salt my side with pity.

I wake with remembrance of Mother in the pub. Mother in the pub and not drinking. Mother, haloed with faint hope and delicious chance for pity laced with sanctimonious solemnity.

"Poor Daughter of mine. How you have fallen. How you have stooped low. Let me help you, my dear. Put your hand in mine. Put my hand on yours."

And if you should push me down with helping, how the more sweet sour.

"I hastened to her side to help, to raise my daughter from the mire." Yet, the hand that went to help could depress as soon as it rose; watch the depravity it beholds, keep it in check, keep it in mire, keep it in control; mother's control.

"Kathleen," she salutes as I turn. "Oh, Kathleen, is this how I find you?"

I look her up and down. I watch the bobbing head. I depart that pub. I know not what she does. I do what she does know. I leave. Again. This time too close for comfort and escape. I only evade the time and day. Inevitable the time we meet again.

Chapter Twenty

"You're drunk," Brigid is shaking me, none too gently, on the sofa.

"I'm not. I'm allergic to her. She brings me out in sweats, hot and dripping. I'm delusional. I'm fucked up. I'm outta here." I struggle to push her off and try to make the door, but Brigid is stronger than she looks and more certain.

"You are not fucked up. You are ok. You hear me, ok?" The last comment is not a question. It is a statement. I am ok, I decide.

That shagging reality TV is on again. I look at my watch. It is a quarter to two. I must have sat and dozed and watched the box for about an hour.

"Are you back on my side again?" I inquire of Brigid. After our last night out, things have been a bit frosty in the house.

"There are things I approve of. And things I don't," she says and will not be drawn further. To be honest, I don't want that conversation in any way, shape or form. I do what I do and if her boyfriend wants to do that too, then that's fine by me. I just don't want the lecture or the talk. Walk a mile in my shoes before you fucking complain about the pinching, sister. Mind you, both Mick and I have been chewed out by our respective partners, and I see no need to sustain secondary injuries.

"So, who is this woman who is bringing you out in cold sweats?" asks Brigid.

I stare at her in amazement. Does she not know? Did I not tell her? My mouth falls open and my chin hits the floor.

"Are you still talking about Marie?"

My chin falls further. I've been talking about Marie? "What are you talking about Brigid?"

It turns out that I have been talking in my sleep a lot. Sometimes, as I sit on the sofa half cut. Sometimes as I lie in my bed and roar at the door. And all this time I thought I was a paragon of discretion. Fuck no. Town crier, more like! How could I have been so vocal? I look at Brigid in amazement. Just what have I been saying? I have to repeat that question, because unusually for me, I didn't say it out loud!

"You think Brent killed Marie. For you. So you could marry."

The fuck I do! Or, maybe, the fuck I do.

The thought that Brent may have killed his sibling, her word not mine, is pretty thrilling. I know I should say chilling, but it is, in all reality, both. Or in all fiction both. I am not sure. It puts an edge on everything I do. On everything I did. On everything he did. On everything he does now.

This thrilling thought lasts all of sixty seconds. Brigid looks at my face and laughs out loud.

"I didn't say he did it, I merely said that you blame him. It's not the same you know, Bella."

I am disgruntled.

"Isn't there enough drama in your life without inventing more?" Brigid asks gently, head perched bird-like on one side.

"He may not have pushed her, but he is responsible as if he had," I contest.

"Maybe," agrees Brigid. "But being responsible for her actions does not make him a killer. And unlikely to come after you. I am less certain about Liam, but then any husband might react in the same way.

Anyway, why do you care so much about her? Surely she meant less than nothing to you? Are you being disingenuous if you say you are upset about someone you actively disliked, about a situation over which you had no control and an outcome that only, subversively, benefited you?"

"God Brigid, stop talking in long sentences and using fucking big words," I collapse back on the sofa.

"Anyway, Mother is here. Here in Ballybawn."

Brigid pauses. Her face is still. "Okay, now I understand. And I am worried too. For all of us." For Brigid to be worried is a worry in itself. I am now officially freaked out.

Chapter Twenty-One

Liam is all excuses. I ring several times and leave messages. I ring another few times and pointedly do not leave messages. Finally I text him to say I am picking him up from his home; where I have to say, he still lives with his parents. That's the trouble with country boys. They still live at home unlike their city cousins. I can understand the food business. Fuck, I can even understand the laundry service. But I cannot get my head around full-blooded males living under Mammy's roof. What the fuck is that all about?

Granted there is not much scope for rental accommodation in the country; I am witness to that, but then the city is limited to those on a budget also. I am tired of fucking in his father's jeep. I am sure his father would be pretty hacked off if he knew also! Actually, that is the one joy of having sex in the jeep—if only his pompous arse of a father knew what his son used the jeep for! Then again, thinking about Tom Dorley and his gross grabs in the pub, perhaps it would turn him on. God, now that turns me off. Right, stinking off.

My text has worked. Liam is on the phone, all excuses. Then angry. He does not know how to apologise; only defend himself. Since the night in the club he has been very distant. It's not the coke. I know that. But I am not sure what is happening. I guess I hoped that once I left Brent we might just take up, properly. But, if anything, it is worse. Before we were excited by the chances we took. Now, Liam is distant. He ebbs and flows. He comes and goes. He is mercurial and moody by turns. When he wants me, it is all want. But when he is finished, it is over. I am getting pissed off. The balance of power is gone, gone in his favour. I don't enjoy this. I am fucked if I am going to stand for it.

Angry Liam cannot meet me this evening. He is busy.

"WHAT THE FUCK IS THIS ALL ABOUT?" I roar down the fucking phone at him. "WE HAVE TO TALK."

He agrees. Anything for a fucking quiet life. Then he says in an almost whisper. "Your mother was here today."

Oh, my fucking shitty life. I have left my psychotic husband, my chicken liver boyfriend is running fast in the opposite direction, and now my mother is dogging my footsteps.

I tell Liam in no uncertain words to fuck right off. The time for talking is well and truly over. I think him the most lily-livered, shitty bastard I have ever had the misfortune to meet, let alone sleep with. I hope he gets genital warts all over his fuck face and lives a miserable fuck lonely life shifting fat women in tight skirts in town, whose beauty is only equaled by his mother's fat arse.

I am not sure how much of my lyrical declamation is heard by Liam because I am spitting down the phone with anger, and when I finally look at the screen the call is ended. By whom I am not sure. But, of course the relationship was ended by mutual consent, fuck off. And that jibe about fat middle-aged, arse-faced women? Be careful what you wish for. That's what they say isn't it?

Chapter Twenty-Two

Work is busy today. There is a buzz. Nicole is marching through the restaurant all pointing and striding about. Arms on hips, checking the décor, the flowers, anyone standing still long enough. She is also very dressed up. Mostly she wears jeans in the morning and changes into smart trousers or a skirt for the evening service. But today she is dressed already.

I am not late, but not early so I don't stop. Instead, I begin checking the orders for the morning; coffee will have to wait. When I get a moment, I ask Tony what is going on. Or rather I raise an eyebrow and look at Nicole. At first he thinks I want to buy. Fuck no, Tony. Not today. I am feeling very mean, and I don't want to do anything when I feel this nasty; it'll only make me worse. Or maybe I do? Anyway, for the moment, I don't. But what the fuck is going on? Obviously my eyebrows are not as expressive as Brigid's!

Turns out a broadsheet supplement is doing a shoot in the restaurant today, interviewing Jeff as they go along. It is considered big news that a hotshot chef should open a very country restaurant and actually run it part-time. It's not the opening per se—quite a few have already done this—but the fact that Jeff actually works here three nights a week.

The photographer arrives shortly, and at first he is very uninspiring. A small little man with a dark shadow, although it is not yet noon. He talks intently to Nicole, who then brings him round the restaurant. To her dismay, he insists on being introduced to all the staff, from cleaners to purchasing officers, aka me! I am sitting when he comes up to me, and I get up deliberately to shake his hand. I may not be dressed to the nines, but my tits are nicely at eye level for Sean, our nice photographer.

And he is nice. He insists on talking to me and seems really interested in my job! He shoots as he talks which is funny because he is not doing the words. My tits are playing a blinder today. I'd love to see the disc for today's shoot; "The Secret World of Bella's Tits' or How to get a set of tits and have them run a restaurant"!

The more he shoots, the more I laugh. Nicole is furious. She tries, unsuccessfully, to deter him to other areas, but he politely refuses to budge. So when I offer him a cup of coffee, he accepts with alacrity. Great, I can piss off Nicole and get my caffeine fix for the morning.

"If you want to finish off your important work, I can look after Sean until Jeff gets in," I smile sweetly at her.

"It's alright…" she begins but Sean cuts her off.

"Thanks Nicole," he says. "I've got enough background shots now and will wait for Jeff as Bella suggests."

I just keep smiling. God, this is fun!

Sean is actually quite funny. Or maybe he's not, but I find myself laughing a lot. That "throw back your head and show off your neck" laughter. Or is that show off my tits? I can't quite tell, but it's making me high, artificially high, and I like it. Easier than snorting a line and much cheaper. I am full on flirting and having a ball. It would appear that Sean is enjoying himself too. He is on his second espresso and shows no sign of moving. Nicole is hovering like a bad dream, always in my peripheral vision, flashing the most vicious looks in my direction. I am going to be in such trouble after but this is worth it.

Good things come to those who wait. Good things come to an end. Which is it to be? Both, in this case as it happens. We wait a long time because Jeff is late and consequently my order was not done. And my good time is definitely over. He bawls me out, Nicole taking the sheepish, tit-filled Sean to other wonders in the restaurant, while I am tongue-lashed by Jeff for every conceivable sin in the culinary planet.

Tongue-lashed by Jeff. There is mastery in his verbiage. Did I mention before that he is loquacious? And do you know, when you don't fucking care about the outcome, then it is interesting and mildly arousing to be bawled out by a man who knows his onions.

I entered work today quite prepared to quit. What was the bloody point? And now, having laughed for an hour in a titillating (oh, that word again!) encounter, I am being given the third degree by Jeff. Should I say his eyes flash and his brow thunders? Not sure, but I am just absorbing his anger; it's professional anger not mere abuse. I must have shown my interest. Perhaps my face smiled or at least I did not look upset enough. He stops mid stream.

"I will finish this later," he snarls. "Try and sort out this mess if you can. I will deal with you when I have finished with this business."

The journalist has also arrived I see, and Jeff readjusts his face to that of friendly civility. I am ignored for the rest of the morning. Nicole makes a point of coming over to me at one point and continues Jeff's rant. However, I raise an eyebrow and carry on working.

"You're not the boss of me," it says. Malcolm in the Middle has some great lines and all I can think of is his mother, Lois I think, and so I just ignore Nicole.

"I'll get Jeff to deal with you later," she echoes parrot-like. Yes please, I think.

"Okay," I say.

But I am not, much to my extreme disappointment, dealt with that afternoon or anytime later. It is almost too much to bear. God, just when I need the distraction, all I get is anticipation without satisfaction. Tony's offer is suddenly very attractive.

That night, Brigid is not wholly unsympathetic. I have not mentioned distractions of course; artificial, photographic, Jeff or Tony's little helper, all she knows is that Liam is off the scene, work is crap, Mother is in town, and Brent appears to be putting her up. Fuck, what happened there? It is Brigid that spills the beans about Mother staying with Brent. I am gobsmacked. Literally. Brigid smacks me in the gob as I start to hyperventilate. I didn't need that Brigid, but I am not surprised by your reaction; it's just there are so many knocks that I can take at once.

I don't believe in fucking fairy tales, but every so often it would be nice to live in a place where things go my way. Fuck you, Liam.

Chapter Twenty-Three

"Just who the fuck was my father?" This time I am screaming it out loud. Mother is temporarily silenced.

We have been at it, hammer and tongs since I arrived at Brent's pub an hour ago. He opened the house door warily and blocked my view, not wanting to grant me access. "I know she is here," I said wearily. And reluctantly he let me pass.

"Who was he? Who is he?" I roar at her again. Her bobbing stops too.

"It is not important," she starts to say, but I cut right across her.

"Not important? Not important? Maybe he could have been the fucking responsible adult when you were wasted and pissed out of your brain," I scream.

Mother sits down heavily on the sofa. I have found her Achilles heel. Only ten years too bloody late.

"It is not important," she begins again.

"What is fucking important then?"

"I have breast cancer. That is important."

I look at her. The begetter of me. But not the betterer of me.

"It all depends on your perspective," I say. I consider turning on my heel and leaving, but something holds me back. Not filial duty, more like curiosity. And I know it killed the fucking cat. "Cancer killed the cat" just doesn't have the same ring. Cancer is killing Mother. Curiosity is killing me. And the cat don't care!

"But why are you here? Why staying with Brent? Are you putting me in your will, just telling me the news or perhaps you were aware that Brent and I have separated? Which is it, Mother?"

Mother raises her hangdog eyes at me. Brent is hovering by the door all this time. I can tell by the way he shifts his feet that he wants to know too. They never met before, my ex-husband and my mother. Isn't it funny how I can turn a man into an ex but not a mother? I declare you my ex-Mother from now on. I can say it, but it doesn't cease to be. She doesn't cease to be. And even when the cancer gets her, she is still my mother in the grave. Spinning in the grave.

"I want to spend my days here," and she gestured grandly if a little sadly round the tiny pub sitting room. "With my daughter and her husband."

I start to laugh. What a mess. Poor Mother can't get it right. "You may not have noticed, Mother, but I don't live here anymore so you can stay wherever you bloody well like. It doesn't bother me."

Brent walks forward angrily. "Your mother. You can't." And I stop him by walking round him and towards the door.

"Just watch me," and I leave.

George is in the car. In the hour that I left him unattended, he has jumped into the front seat and chewed the old leather steering wheel. Be the fuck. How can a dog be so stupid? There are great big welts in the wheel and lumps on the seat. I start to scream again. This time abuse at the dog. I larrup him hard across his haunches. Three times. Of course, he probably hasn't chewed for the past twenty minutes and hasn't a fucking clue why I am a raving loony. I rest my head on the mangled steering wheel and draw breath.

Finally "Let's walk," I say.

Up in the forest all is quiet. George does his fucking lunatic act, running at speeds a greyhound would envy. Then, he returns near me and begins sniffing with vast excitement a spot by the path. I have no idea what it is, but his whole body is quivering with excitement. His tail wags his body. His tail is a dangerous weapon. His body is one long tail. Swish wag, swish wag. His bloodhound lineage is obvious in his sniffing, and I can hear the snortled breathy sound from his loose skin round his muzzle.

It quivers and flaps hollowly through the heavy intake of scent and air.

I walk over to take a look, but the hot gossip that George can read is blank to me. He looks up at me momentarily before resuming his frenzied smelling.

I walk. I walk on. I walk on by. George runs. George runs on. George runs on by. I walk faster, but not as fast as George.

I return to the question in hand. Just who was my father? Somehow this seems more important than the fact of my mother's impending death. Mama, we all go to hell. Mama, we are all gonna die. The fact that hers may be nearer than expected is immaterial to me.

I walk faster, but not as fast as George.

Why was Brent putting Mother up? She obviously did not know we had separated when she came but still, Brent and Mother? I cannot see them eating breakfast together. Not watching telly in the evening. Or passing each other on the stairs.

"After you, please." "No, no, I insist, after you." And my darling alcoholic mother sleeping in a pub? Not the best of situations.

I walk faster, but not as fast as George.

Maybe Mother could convert Brent? Or Brent bed Mother? Now, I start to laugh at the absurdity of it. But in my mind's eye I can see it. Horrible fucking pictures come unbidden into my head. It is like a film, black and white, a newsreel, playing in my head. I hear the music, the melodrama. He towers over her. The music swells loudly. He flings back an arm; he is wearing a cape, and it floods backwards. She falls against the chair. Arm raised in fear, or is it excitement? He is over her, bearing down on her. Encompassing her. The cape falls across them, coyly, but not before I see the glint in her eye. Brent is fucking Mother.

I stop. It is too steep. My nose is running, and my eyes are tearing. I start to cry. I cry. I cry on. I cry on by. George, thank the fuck, does not cry. But he stops too. Hears my keening. Stops and turns and runs to me. Launches himself at me.

"Down George," I shout through my snotty nose and running tears and keening cries. He pays no attention and launches himself again at me. He almost knocks me down. His paw prints are all over me. I am then pushed down. Or else I just sit. I cannot say for sure. George is now on top and in control. His paws are on my shoulder. I am covered in wet fucking mud. He licks my face as if it were an ice cream.

"Oh George," I say. Words are not enough. Words do not mean anything to George. He just is. Right now, he just is fucking filthy. I am fucking filthy. But really, Brent is not fucking Mother.

"Brent is not fucking your mother," echoes Brigid. The fact that she curses stops me in my rant. "But you are filthy. Go and take a hot shower,"

"What? And risk electrocuting myself?"

"If necessary,"

I have stopped walking. But George is still faster.

Chapter Twenty-Four

I am asleep when my mobile goes off. It is a text. What time
is it? I look at the phone. Only ten thirty. But then I drank a
bottle of wine very fast and went to bed at nine. I open the
flip phone and select the inbox. In the dark of my bedroom
the light is very bright. The text, white on a blue background,
is livid. One new message. From Liam. I look for a moment
at his name. Dumbly. I wonder why he is writing to me. What
does he want to say? I stare at the inbox and his name, and I
debate if I should open it or delete it. Naturally, curiosity gets
the better of me.

"Babe"

One word. I look at it in wonder. What does it mean?
What the fuck does it mean? Of course, I know what the fuck
it means. Like a zombie I get out of bed and pull on my
clothes. I am on autopilot. I touch my face but decide I don't
need makeup. It is dark out for God's sake. We don't meet in
public. Even now. Not in the village. What am I talking
about? We are over. We are not an item anymore. I sit down
on the bed and pick up the phone again. I opened his text. It
glows in the darkness.

Then another text arrives. Also, from Liam. I look at
the new one critically. As if I can tell what it says just by
looking at his name. Then I open it too.

"Babe"

He has sent the same fucking text again to see if he can get a reaction. He can't be bothered to come up with a new thought or text. He is relying on the old code words from our relationship to trigger my response. And it is fucking working.

Quickly, before I change my mind, I reply, "Where?"

"Baileys Bridge" is the response. Like a speed dial he must have been waiting for the positive.

When I arrive, he is parked under the bridge. The lights are off, but I can see the glow from his cigarette. I pull up beside him and turn off my engine. I look at my battered and chewed steering wheel for a moment. Then I open my door and climb out to meet my lover. A lovers' tryst. Except there are no flowers.

He puts out his cigarette. Flicks it out the window of the jeep.

"Your mother," he begins but I cut him short. I literally lean over and kiss the words out of him. I don't want to fucking talk about my mother. I don't want to think about my mother. I don't want to think, period.

He pulls me towards him, pulls me on top of him. We are so urgent, we bang teeth. Ordinarily this would make me laugh, but I am too intent on kissing him. It is too intense. His hands pull me, paw me, cover me, undress me, clumsily. I am awkward too. Months of doing it in a jeep has not finessed our ability to undress with any degree of ease in the front seat.

I rear up, panting. "Let's get in the back," I say. I look in and it is filled with clutter. "Fuck you, Liam. Did you ever think to toss out some of the fucking shit in the jeep?" I am angry. I am aroused. I am both.

Liam looks into the back also. "I can sort it," he says and climbs in. It is like a comedy. He fires clothes, boots, and garden tools to one side. He makes a hollow. He lies back in it and smiles.

I smile too and climb in.

It is intense, and it is over very quickly. I lay back panting.

His eyes are closed. "Babe," he says.

Our code word. Our tryst in the back of a cluttered jeep. Right now, I am high. I am exhilarated. I touch his body. He quivers. He is like George. Wagged by his tail also.

I touch his body. He is incarnate. He is corporal. He is incandescent.

I touch his body. Stroke his chest. Trail my fingernails across his belly. His skin is white. I am reminded of the gamekeeper. White and hidden from the sun. He opens his eyes momentarily. And does his laugh. It is half chortle, half laugh. It is pure enjoyment. It makes me smile too. He is ticklish. He closes his eyes again.

Right now, I am all. I am whole. I am content. I am. I nestle up close and trace my fingers on his chest. Breathe into him. Breathe him into me. His arm is around me. We are in embrace. We are in tryst.

"Babe" he says again and drifts off.

I don't sleep, but I lie content. An hour passes. He opens one eye. His humour has changed. Ticklish is gone, and he is jokey instead. Jocular and keen to be gone.

I try to hold him. To trace him with my caress. To bind him with my touch. To hold back the tide, but I may as well be King Canute. He slips away like quicksilver. I put out my hands and try to catch the elusive essence, but even as I watch, he pours through my fingers like sand. There is only the memory left. Like a sulphurous trace.

I look at my hands. Hands that held him, touched him. Hands that traced his face. Curved round his belly. Etched their imprint on his back. Grasped his buttocks.

My hands are empty now and he is gone. Smoking a cigarette outside the jeep. I pull on my hastily discarded clothes. I take my keys. I look at Liam. He makes a move to come closer, but I raise my hands. Back off they say. Those empty hands.

"Your mother," he says again, and I almost fucking kick him in the bollox.

I get in my car and drive off. I curse all the fucking way home. I have so many put downs for that fucking low life. I am tempted to turn around and tell him. When I get home I am tempted to ring him, text him, I have such scathing remarks I want to make. George greets me in the doorway. Brigid is just coming in. Mick is with her. She looks at me.

"You didn't?" she says, with her eyebrow raised, in a disappointing kind of way.

"I fucking did," I answer, and Mick looks at both of us in query.

"Ah, sure," she says. "Let there be no drama. As Sonia's Dad once said – Is anyone dead? I think not. Let's chalk this up to the …" and she casts around for an excuse."

"The moon," says Mick helpfully. "It's almost full tonight." He looks at both of us brightly.

I look out the doorway to the full moon. It is white and translucent as his skin. I look at my hands. They are still empty. I hold them up and frame the moon.

"Yes, the moon is a good excuse." And now I have a month to repair myself before it fills again.

Chapter Twenty-Five

Work is shite boring. It is Thursday, and Jeff is up in his Dublin emporium. Nicole remains in the country. She lives here now and only goes to Dublin on her days off. I personally cannot see the attraction. I mean why live in this Godforsaken hole when she could be up in Dublin. And what about Jeff, what does he do when he is not in the country? It is like the town mouse and the country mouse, only I reckon the town mouse gets up to a lot more than was ever covered in the fairy tale. Okay, that's just my febrile imagination.

I personally cannot see the attraction. That is Nicole I mean. She is like a scalded cat and twice as mean. She flicks her long straight blond hair like a midget with St Vitus's dance. Did I say she was short? Hell, yes. All boobs and dinky legs and pert behind like a tiny European gymnast. She walks like a gymnast also, dainty steps, legs flicked out in front, toes almost pointing in her tiptoppy shoes. But her arms swing menacingly. Like she is winding herself up to launch into a cartwheel in the air. The power in those puny limbs is quite shocking. I've seen her lug heavy boxes around and her biceps ping like hard limes.

Jeff picks her up, almost. His hands circle her waist. They span it with ease. She is like a child then, tippy toeing in her ridiculous heels. She coos then—fuck, that's where he gets it from—and doe-eyes him. It's enough to make me puke.

And if Nicole with Jeff is painful, without him she is even worse. Forget the cooing and tippy toeing, she is a hundred percent Russian gymnast. Or rather the Russian gymnastic team's coach.

Today in my shite day, Nicole makes a point of making sure I feel doubly shite. I am given the task of stocktaking all the dry goods in the walk-in food store. It was only done a few weeks ago, but no, it has to be done again, from scratch and finished by lunchtime.

I do it.

Then she hands me the paperwork for the quarter and asks me to categorise it according to product, to supplier, to quantities. Then I am to check for price fluctuations, outside of seasonal or weight differences, and report back on any variations.

I do it

Then she asks me to clean the toilets. I look at her and am about to fucking explode when she laughs.

"Oh Bella," she says. "Your face is priceless."

Fuck off Nicole. Fuck off country mouse. I fuck off too. Home. I ignore Tony's invitation. I can't be fucking arsed to do anything. I want out of this hell hole.

Brigid is home early. Clutching a load of papers.

"Homework," she says but when I look at the copy books, it is all tumultuous writing from tiny hands. 'The leaves are brown in autumn,' they say. All curvy vowels and fat consonants. And lines that dip above and below the lined paper. Breathless writing with great big splodges for full stops, when pencils have been pushed mercilessly into the paper, and sometimes through the paper, to make the period.

I am lethargic. I am bored. I want Brigid to come and play.

"Bella wants to play with Brigid," I say. Brigid looks sadly at me.

"Maybe later when I am finished," she says.

"No, now. Bella wants to play now," I shout. I stomp around the room. George jumps with me. "We want to play now," I shout, and George barks.

"Oh, for God's sake, Bella, would you ever shut up."

George and I ignore Brigid. George and Bella play. We knock over the lamp and the bulb crashes. George yelps and backs off. Bella just laughs. Brigid gives up and moves her work into the kitchen.

George looks at Bella. Bella looks at George. Fuck this, for a game of soldiers.

Bella is off to the pub. George looks at Bella. "You can't come my old fucker," Bella says. "They don't allow dogs in the pub. You'd only knock over things and get sick all over the floor. You can leave that to me instead."

"For Christ's sake," yells Brigid from the kitchen. "Would you ever give over and get out? Give me some peace."

George says, "I'll be good if I am allowed to come." Bella looks at George. "You didn't really say that, did you?" she asks. In response, George just grins enigmatically.

"Get out," screams Brigid, "before you do my head in."

Bella scrams. George stays, and Brigid breathes a sigh of relief.

Chapter Twenty-Six

I am treading water. I am very good at treading water. I should have drowned long ago, but some primitive instinct keeps me afloat. I am not sure how, but the instinct to survive is very strong. I swim among sharks and surface unscathed. Or perhaps I have become the shark? Perhaps I was always the impostor, like the ugly duckling.

Turn that story around and you have a very different tale. Lazy swan parent deposits needy child in duck nest.

"You bring the brat up, you stupid duck," sneers Mother Swan swimming quickly away. Ugly duckling may never match up to her adopted, impostored-upon, siblings, but she is bigger. So she bullies, shouts and stomps her way through hormone propelled weeks. Other pretty duck siblings cower before her. Mother Duck is also quickly dwarfed by blundering teenage daughter; the long neck arches when angry, the wings flap frighteningly; the legs are boned and tough.

"Don't mess with me, Mother," flaps ugly duckling and Mother Duck doesn't.

Mother Swan returns six weeks later, Claims her own and they all live happily ever after. Except ugly duckling has a complex about her size. Her thinner, slighter siblings have always made her feel awkward and clumsy. Forget the smooth image of graceful swans on top and legs swishing furiously below—oh, not for ugly duckling. She grew up big and bold and now she is with her elegant Mother Swan she feels small and vulnerable. Rejected and hurt. She bullied her adoptive mother but cannot do the same to her birth mother.

Except, I never had adoptive siblings or even an adoptive mother. All I had was my own birth mother, whom I am sure would have left me in a duck nest had one been handy.

"I have been given between three and six months," Mother tells me. We are sitting in the main bar. I refuse to sit in the living room out back. I have left and don't want to go back. I also want a drink.

I look at her, and I just wonder why. Why is Mother dying of cancer? Why now? Why has she come back? What does she want from me?

She reads my mind. "I want to help you, Kathleen," she says. "That's why I am here. There is a reason for my cancer, and it is to help you." She glances back towards the bar where Brent is talking to a punter. "And help that lovely man too."

I almost choke on my pint. I start laughing once I recover. She is not amused. Her mouth purses, sharp and tight.

"I am not happy with your situation," she says. "If I hadn't gotten my life sentence, I never would have sought you out. I wouldn't have known what you were doing—this life you're throwing away. I think you need to think very carefully about your decision."

Yeah, yeah. I nod enough to keep her going and totally tune out. Mother talks on and I just don't listen. It is all irrelevant. I look curiously but idly over at Brent. He has stopped talking to the customer and is now watching us intently, straining as if to hear what is being said. I expect they have rehearsed much of what is coming out of her mouth now. Thought of all the angles, the reasons, the rationales.

I look back at Mother and nod again. I watch her mouth moving. It opens and closes, and words come out like bubbles. They hover for a moment in front of her face before moving off, followed by the next series of bubbles. Some are clear, some have colour, some spin as they move. As they leave her mouth, they begin to lose their texture, their shape, their gloss. Then, rather than popping like real bubbles, they just vanish. Vapourise. Disappear. Vamoose!

I drink again. But the drink is not making the bubbles. They just are. They just are there. There.

Then I become aware that her words are not the only things creating bubbles. As I watch, I see her body has an echo. It is fine and wispy, attached loosely with thin threads that sway in her warmth. It is red around her head but becomes purple as it stretches down her body. She moves and it moves with her, with a slight delay, like a visual echo.

"Have you heard a word I have said?," says Mother, actually sounding like a real mother. Like I imagine concerned Mother Duck would have asked of me. Mother Swan would not give a flying fuck and would be too busy swanning around with Mr Swan, Daddy Swan perhaps, or just Mr Current Swan. Fuck, I am really confusing my metaphors.

Am I swan, ugly duckling or shark? Is Mother Duck Mother or Swan Mother? Fuck if I know.

All I do know is that it is much more fun trying to figure out who is who, than listening to the sanctimonious drivel coming out of my mother's mouth. It is no longer bubbles but spewing waves of dripping fog. It belches out in green waves, undulating and rolling across her chin before it spills down her chest, splashing great big puddles on her chest before poof! it too vapourizes. Except it leaves a slight, greenish stain on her chin and jumper. And it smells slightly, like stale water left in a vase.

I leave the pub. I put down my drink, still only one drink, despite the colour coded excretions now flooding out of Mother and put on my coat. She is furious and spits out her words. I don't listen to them. I don't have to. They are all there in glorious technicolour in front of me. I step backwards. I don't want them staining me, marking my clothes, marking me, leaving stains. Out! damn mark. Out damn spot. Fuck if I'm going to let her mark me, stain me, spot me.

As I leave I look at Brent. He has no colour but a sliver, shiver of ice blue covers him, blurs him. It looks clean and crisp, but he is hard to see through the pane of frozen water. He is blunted and blurred through the sharpness.

Now, make no mistake, he is shark.

Chapter Twenty-Seven

Brigid insists. "You must speak with her," she says. "You can't ignore it, her or him. These are all things that must be dealt with. They won't go away, in fact I suspect they will only get worse if you ignore them."

Bella doesn't agree. Bella sulks. Bella raises her eyes and ignores Brigid.

"If you start that malarkey again, I shall hit you," Brigid says, but Bella continues to ignore her.

Still, Brigid's words must have sunk in because here I am in my old marriage bedroom looking for something. I don't know what I am looking for. It could all be a dream for all I really know. I look in my old chest of drawers, but they are as empty as I left them. Brent has not moved his stuff into my empty space, but then his possessions were always very sparse. He never had more clothes than he needed. If he bought a new shirt, then an old one went out. Underwear was updated on a regular basis. Folded with military precision in his drawers, lined up for a full military parade. He hated my mess and

I revelled in it, especially when it riled him.

I move from my old bedroom to the guest room. I am glad to see that Mother's things are all here, and nowhere else. Her bed is made. There is a different bed spread out. I preferred the black Chinese quilt, but Mother has replaced that with a striped pastel affair. I think it was a wedding present from a supplier to the pub. I hated the thing but I am not surprised that Mother likes it. I walk around the room, like a somnambulant. I look at her things, but I don't touch them. She has brought a surprising amount of luggage with her. Even boxes and cartons. She has obviously no intention of moving on soon. I wonder that Brent isn't more worried about her invasion. This is no ordinary visit. She has come to die. Her things will be littered here after she is gone.

But then, I am pleased that all her worldly goods are here. I suddenly know what I am after - the shoe box. A shabby shoe box that served as a repository for an eclectic selection of papers, all loved or important to my mother. Brigid sowed the seed in me. Not that she intended to. Brigid thought she was sowing the seed of reconciliation in me, of compassion, of love. But that seed fell on stony ground. No, the seed I nurtured was that of discovery. I planted that thought, that idea, and it sprang forth with energy. So much so, that here I am. Let in by my old, unreturned house key, and standing like a thief in the day in my old house.

I move from foot to foot. Balancing myself. Pausing for a moment before I reach out and touch the uppermost carton. I almost shock myself. I jolt. I tremble. But the carton does not jolt or shock me back. It is all in my head. Or rather, in my fingers that transmit this nervous energy back to my body. I open the lid of the carton, but there is no shoe box on view, just, strangely, hair nestling on cloth. I step back, this time with reason. What is she doing with hair in a carton? Then I consider her condition and the fact that it might be a wig. I am not sure, but I will not touch it. I shake the carton from the sides, and the hair slides quickly to reveal books beneath. The cloth appears to be a scarf of some kind. The books I see are all religious.

It's like a quest on the telly. One of those mad Japanese game shows—so loved and ridiculed by the likes of Chris Tarrant and Clive James—long before the English came up with their own brand of tacky voyeurism in those endless reality programmes I hate but still end up watching all the same.

Here I am in my very own reality show. Can Bella find the treasure box without touching anything belonging to her mother? What will be in the other boxes? Spare livers to replace the cancerously mutating organ that she carries? It is killing her from the inside, sludging up her insides so the green gloup pours from her liver into the surrounding tissues, poisoning all in its ambit. But then, Mother was always very good at the poison. It is not mere coincidence that I call myself Bella, my chosen name, my given path. From Bella Donna, the deadly nightshade that once was used to redden lips. Deadly the kiss received from lips that stung red.

The tension mounts. I am opening boxes and looking inside. I am opening luggage and checking the contents. The clock is ticking. I hear the commentator caution me.

"Hurry up," he says. "Your time is running out. Your time is nearly up."

"But my time is now," I want to reply. "I am taking my time. I am staking my time. I am raking my time. It is my time."

Then suddenly, jackpot! I look under the bed, and there is the shoe box. I pause, and the crowd goes wild. I hear the commentator try and talk over the cheers.

"Bella has found the box," he repeats. "She has found the box."

But no one is listening. They are all too busy jumping and shouting and clutching each other with joy.

"Bella has found the box," he repeats.

The pause is no longer artificial. It is real. I actually stop and pause. Then, what the fuck, I open the shoe box. I know what I want to find. I want my birth certificate. I remember it being here before. It must be here. It is here. Kathleen Mary Brown. God help me, what a fuck awful name! No wonder I changed it. No wonder I christened myself. Parents should not be allowed to name their children. What the fuck was my mother thinking when she gave me that spineless name.? It should be mandatory for parents to review their children's names at teenagehood. Let the kids fucking choose I say. And then again when we get older, let's change again. The same name cannot be suitable for a lifetime. Our bodies change, our faces change, our personalities change, so why not our names?

And there on the right-hand side of the certificate is my father's name. Conrad George Creighton. I did not expect it to be there. I expected nothing or unknown. You bitch Mother, you knew that this might cause trouble later on and you made sure to record his name. Bitch Mother I salute you for once. Now fuck off and die. Oups, that's what you're going to do. Sigh.

Chapter Twenty-Eight

It appears that I am flavour of the month after all. Not with the Russian dwarf, of course. But Jeff is uncommonly civil. He seems to have forgotten his anger from the day of the shoot, but that is his style. He conforms to celebrity chef in a number of ways, his sudden outbursts being one aspect.

He has thrown knives in the kitchen, literally. A busboy clumsy enough to back into him during service was the unlucky recipient of a flying knife, almost; he knocked into Jeff causing him to throw au jus all over the plates in front of him. It wasn't the careful tracing of his signature dish, but a mess of red sauce squeezed with all the skill of a tomato ketchup splash. Jeff roared with anger, red colour rushing up his cheeks, and spun round.

The busboy compounded matters by not noticing what he had done and continued carrying his heavy tray of dirty dishes to the sink. Jeff put his hand on a knife that lay beside him. An innocent knife with a wicked blade. He balanced it in his hand for a moment, and before sense could check his actions, flung it over to the sink. It missed the busboy, mercifully though by luck or good judgment no one was sure and clattered harmlessly to the ground. The busboy put his hand to his head, feeling in retrospect the rushing air that carried that knife past his left ear, frighteningly close to his left ear, but fortunately not coming into contact with his left ear, even in the action replay.

Even in the pub that night, it never found its mark, despite thrilling the stilled kitchen as it spun like a silver arrow in its arcing trajectory, just missing that left ear, much valued by the owner, who probably heard the swish as it sliced through the air, but fortunately not through his ear.

As the clatter hung in the air, Jeff turned back to two covers, ruined, in front of him. He ordered up two fresh orders, checked the jus remaining in the pan, and continued as if nothing had happened. And nothing had, except it was the busboy's last day, in his current job. But not his last day on this earth, thank the fuck.

My popularity today turns out is all to do with my tits. Well, of course, they are a considerable source of popularity in many circles, but on this occasion, the circles in question are very important circles or rather they move in very important circles, whatever. An asset is an asset, is an asset. And these puppies are certainly an asset.

It is Sean firstly, my friendly photographer, who latched onto my tits. He was just the right height to appreciate them. And he gave them plenty of airtime in his pictures. Then the editor liked the shots when laying out the feature. It has two pages and six pictures, and I am in three of them. That's only one less than Jeff and it was his piece after all.

Jeff tells me this with a half-smile playing on his lips. What a strange expression that is, playing on his lips. What was the half smile playing? The banjo, perhaps? I can't imagine it would be a serious instrument like the piano or a tuba. Or perhaps the half smile is not playing a musical instrument after all. Perhaps it is playing a joke, a round of golf, or just plain playing hard to get.

I find this whole line of thought so funny that I crack up. Jeff is totally bemused. He has no idea of the depths to which my mind will descend. I am now officially on Planet Ridiculous. It makes it easier, therefore, when he leans forward and kisses me. Makes it easier for me to kiss him back. Makes it easier for me to ignore the fact we are in the office with the door only slightly closed. Or only slightly open depending on whether you are entering or leaving. We are not leaving, but someone is entering.

Jeff, obviously trained in kissing pretty girls in unsafe locations, is cool as a fucking cucumber. He leans back and pulls open a drawer in the filing cabinet. He makes the move in a seamless way as if he was in the process of doing this when the door swung open. I, not to be beaten in the fucking cool cucumber stakes, remain still. I do not jump up, move back or even look round. I wait until Jeff greets Nicole, of course it is Nicole, that I look over my shoulder at her, but say nothing. I am in a meeting, my face says. My face is bland. She, Nicole, is not bland at all. But there is nothing for her to attack.

"Do you want to look at the specials now," she says, looking at Jeff but sending poison arrows in my direction.

I, Bella Donna, am immune to such barbs. They bounce off me like tiny spears might tickle Gulliver in Lilliput.

Jeff says yes. Dismisses me to my chagrin. My fucking chagrin.

Chapter Twenty-Nine

Brent is at the door. Fuck me. Don't let that show on my face. "Hello Brent." He stands there, and I stand here. I don't move to one side. I don't invite him in. He does not step forward. This is my ground. My space. My water.

He is shark. He is circling and now he thinks he can smell blood. I see his white belly arch with excitement. He extends. He is about to twist on his back and slowly, relentlessly rush his prey. His cold eyes appraises the space. If he flips now and turns on his back, one swish of his tail and he is beside me, his recessed mouth and teeth will open and separate a piece of flesh from my body. Shearing silently in the water, there will be no sound. Even the bubbling blood will spread across the water in silence, no dripping noise, no tearing, ripping sounds, just flesh pulled from flesh, from bone, and leaking, pouring blood across the water, all in silence. In space, who will hear you scream?. In water who will hear you tear, rip, flesh from flesh?.

All I see are his eyes.

He gestures to the road.

"Let us walk," he says without moving his lips. Walking is preferable to swimming, to drowning, to dying, and I accept his gesture. Wordlessly.

We walk. We never walked before. Our patterns are all wrong. Our feet march to different drums. It is stop, start, stop, muddle through. Walking is still preferable to moving through water. My feet are on terra firma. I can feel the ground beneath my feet.

Brent is talking, I think. I have developed profound deafness. An inability to hear. A thickness that is akin to swimming underwater. Muffled and muted, sound travels in waves and all is distorted and broken up. I catch the odd word and sense his meaning, but not his intent. Or rather his intent is so sharp, it incises me, cuts me, eviscerates me as I walk.

He is moving now in water. I am becoming afraid. The ground beneath my feet is bending and undulating. The wind is becoming waves. I am not walking anymore but moving through water, slowly. First my feet miss the ground, then my legs are pulled back through the surge of water, then my arms feel the heaviness of air becoming water. My lungs strain to pull in air, oxygen. Water rushes where air flowed before. In my terror, I look over at Brent. Our missed steps are not obvious now that sluggishness pulls them into pattern. The drum, if ever heard, is muffled in the water that is swirling around us, and the beat is thump, thump, thump, echoed and distant and hollow.

> Like a submerged bell rocked on a sunken galleon. The drum is my heartbeat and even that is distant from me. I am floating now, but in weariness. Heavy, yet supported by the water. What is to come next? I am resigned. I am weary. I am drowning if I but knew it. In ignorance I look over at Brent. I half expect him to be covered in dripping, waving seaweed, but he is

not vegetable; he is animal, he is fish, he is shark. He is smiling.

His smile grows, Cheshire like, until it fills his face. His eyes are creased and closed to slits. His smile is full, thin, wide and horrible. His smile is his face. He looks at me. His eye grows thinner still as it sizes me. Sizes me—and finds me wanting, finds me wasting, finds me flesh. He flips onto his back, white belly upturned and glistening in the water. He shifts his body from side to side, effortlessly cutting through the cold water, the ice-cold water. He pushes up to me and opens his maw. The cutting rows of teeth all bared and ready to tear my flesh from my bone. He opens his maw, his jaw, and bites.

Liam is seeing Fiona Jennings. Ten years his senior. Ten years mine. Ten pounds heavier and ten inches shorter. Escorting her around the village, in open view of all.

Flesh cut from me. You bastard Brent. Sharks kill and maim and injure for the blood. Food is not the only point. Blood floating on the water is just enough. You saw my blood. My potential for blood. Your revenge was very swift and very cruel.

Drowning and not waving at all, except like a fool to the lifeguard. But where the fuck, who the fuck is the lifeguard?

Chapter Thirty

I am putting on makeup badly. My hands are trembling and
my movements awkward. My face, my face of twenty-three
years, suddenly seems alien to me. I don't recognise the nose.
The eyes are horribly different, slit eyes, chink eyes. My
forehead seems to have grown to Quasimodo proportions.
And my hair falls lank, lacklustre and down.

Makeup will not work. I look blankly at the makeup
on my dressing table. It will not do. It will not do at all. Short
of a paper bag, I cannot leave this house and be seen in
public. I crash out of my room and search the bathroom, but
there is no makeup there. I am looking wildly through the
cabinet, chucking bottles and jars on the floor when Brigid
walks in.

She looks at me. At my face. At what my face is
screaming at her.

"I know," she says. "I heard already,"

"You knew?" I am very angry. Angrier than when I
discovered the features on my face resembled a scrapbook
collage. Very angry.

"I should have told you, but I didn't know how. It
was all so sudden, and I hoped it would pass or … you would
pass on him," Brigid's voice ran out. She looked at me
apologetically.

"I just didn't want to tell you the bad news. I reckoned you had enough on your plate."

I groan. Anger leaves me quickly. "Instead, you left it for Brent to tell me," I whisper in anguish. "Brent of all people for fuck's sake. He even had the balls to ask if we could give it another shot. Or rather he said that he would take me back, forgive me my sins, my transgressions."

"He's spending a lot of time with your mother."

The statement hangs in the air and I don't have to answer. Time with the cloth has given Mother a language of her own laced with divine clearance. Brent, no stranger to adopting stances that suit his purpose, has obviously charged himself with righteousness rigor. For a man that hated the church with a vengeance, his adoption of the church and its language might be seen as a surprise if nothing else. But for a man who was fucking his sister, he has a fucking cheek. I am incensed and frightened at the same time.

I look at Brigid.

"He said there would be repercussions if I did not come back. He is very angry. He does not let things go."

"It is all threats." Brigid speaks very deliberately and slowly. "He cannot touch you. You have left him. It is over."

I don't know. I don't know if I believe her. I know I want to believe her, but Brent is a law unto himself. Brent's law. The world according to Brent. Brent and the law. Each world is only that which it touches. Some worlds are very tiny. Actually, most worlds are not that big. How many people does Brent touch, really? How many do I? We can all be potentates in our own little worlds. Wreck havoc with our rules and strictures on our members; terrorise with feudal authority and arrogance. Our world, our rules, our dictates.

And in each world, like a replica of the globe, each rule is bent and subjected to the ruling power. With what mirror can you check the sanity of sense? If all is bent and curved, like a fairground attraction mirror, then how can we tell the rule from the ruler?

What is the price of leaving Brent's world? I genuinely don't fucking know. Did Marie pay the ultimate price? Did she fuck him, then fuck him, then fuck off him. Did she know what she was doing? Did she step out of his world and fall, fall into a worldless state, a state of nothingness? Or did she step into the light?. God help the poor bitch, I don't think she had a clue. Her rules, governed by her fairground mirror, were not his. She was not potentate, at all. At least not in his world and that was where she lived. Big mistake, sister.

Brigid touches me. She holds my face and looks into my eyes. Her hands are warm and soft.   "Whatever is going on in your mind, let me tell you, it is okay. You are okay." Her breath is warm and soft.

My features all soften and fall into place. I am not Picasso's cartoon muse after all. I am fucking okay.

"Let's go face that world," she says.

We go where we know Liam will be. It is a small village after all and options are limited. I am prepared. I have been through much worse. I am fucking sex on legs. This much is borne out by the looks and interest I generate. Why did I fucking doubt myself earlier?

I am so cool. I am fucking on fire. I am an ice bitch. I am hot, hot, hot. I am fucking flipflopping, but no one fucking knows. Except maybe Brigid. Except definitely Brigid.

It must be the oldest, most frustrating question in the world, but why not me? Why Fiona? I really can't stand this. Liam is a fucking headless fucking shit. He won't look in my direction, except under hooded eyes. Fiona is riding her wave and not paying me any attention, her hiny perched on the bar stool, and legs crossed and tapping crossly. Her tune. Her rules, maybe. Don't get too comfortable bitch because I see his eyes move. I know how they move. Eyes front, eyes first, eyes follow, eyes robbing the sight, eyes robbing, eyes robin, cock robin, cock rubbing me up. Who killed Cock Robin?

There is a lull in the noise. It is twenty past the hour? I was told once that lulls are caused by angels moving through the room, at twenty past or twenty to the hour. The lull is a stillness; a lessening in the clamour in the room. A stillness settling across the room, across the faces made yellow by the lights. Mouths close and breaths exhale, softly. I can't see the angels but I sense their movement, their presence, a trace on my retina, a memory, a flash of brightness captured on the inside of my eyes, in the dark cupped hollows of my sockets.

In the still, the eternal pause, the quiet moment, I look over at Liam and our eyes link, connection made, and sudden lust darkens his eyes. It is only a moment and even as we both look away, the angels leave and sound pours back into the pub like a wave; a cresting, noisy, splashing wave. Mouths open at once and suck in the noise, spitting it out, coughing it out, shouting it out, shrieking it out in raucous laughter.

I am too tired, there, it is done. Brigid, God bless her cotton picking socks, understands instantly. We leave. I am content with the direct result of being there, attracting attention, looking good, playing the part, and now leaving early.

Later, I get into bed. Turn off the light. I am satisfied to a point. Then my mobile goes. Flashes in the dark. It is Liam.

"Babe" the message reads. After a moment's hesitation, I delete it.

Who killed Cock Robin? You did Liam with your fucking bow and arrow. You killed Cock Robin.

Chapter Thirty-One

The king is dead! Long live the king! Same principle applies to domestic pets; dogs, cats, hamsters, though possibly not goldfish. Actually, with goldfish, replacement need not even come with discovery. Overall, it's a good principle and a sound one. Shame it cannot be applied to family. The mother is dead! Long live the mother!

My mother is now door stepping me. It would be very funny if it were not so horribly fucked up. I leave the house, and she is there. I catch a bus, and she is on it. I go to work, and she is at the diner. By herself, always. But her fingers are draped with her rosary beads. Clicking and clacking, as she moves. She cannot stalk me in the dark because I can hear her coming. As I leave work, sometimes walking, in the dark, I hear her behind me. Moaning entreaties and click, clacking her beads.

"Go home, Mother," I say but all I get by return is "Child of Grace, talk to me."

"Eh, no, Mother. I have nothing to say to you."

How fucking unlucky I am. After all the crap I have put up with in my fucked-up life so far, my own mother is now haunting me while still alive. How fucking fucked-up is that, am I?

"Talk to her," insists Brigid but I am as stubborn as my mother.

"Bella doesn't want to talk to Mother," I repeat sulkily and Brigid, totally pissed off with me, changes the subject. Utterly.

The natural order of things; one following another, one replacing another, one tagging another, holds true for most. But the act of natural succession cannot apply to Mothers, there being only one of course and even in the best of syrupy movies stepmums do not really cut the mustard. In the natural order of things, one king follows another, as night follows day, winter follows autumn and decay follows death; or is it death following decay, spring following winter and day following night?

The affair is over! Long live the affair! I am ready to be changed. Change the subject Brigid. Change the lover, Bella. Change the record Mother.

I am ready to be seduced. Or to seduce. I cannot decide which excites me more.

Chapter Thirty-Two

"What do you read?"

"I don't"

"You must read something, even if it is only the sports pages, the horoscopes, the back of a milk carton over breakfast."

"I don't read on principle, at all," I insist. "Except, perhaps tea leaves."

Jeff laughs. He is leaning over me in the office where I am furiously working through my paperwork. I have not turned around. I am pretending to work now. Pen in hand, scanning the pages in front of me. I am not going to look around. Jeff places both hands on my shoulders. I feel the warmth of his flesh through my shirt. His hands are moving, massaging gently, rolling the skin and muscle through the thin cloth.

"Don't you mean bags?" he suggests.

"Bags?"

"Yeah, tea bags. No one uses tea leaves anymore. So, you must read the teabags."

I stifle a giggle.

"Maybe," I agree. "But I slit them open like a chicken's gizzard and investigate the leaves properly."

"I bet you do," Jeff laughs. "But I think you are mistaking tasseography for voodoo."

In a slick movement, he slips a hand down the front of my shirt. I am so taken aback I stop breathing and freeze. His hand cups my breast and rubs the nipple through my bra. Then he pushes the material up and his flesh is touching my flesh.

This is not what I want. Actually, this is what I want, but not the way I want it. I stand up and Jeff is taken off guard. He pulls his hand out of my clothes, and I straighten myself. Then slowly turning round, I look him in the eye. We are the same height, or rather in my heels, we are the same height.

"I do want you," I say looking straight at him. Now, back in balance again, Jeff smiles. I continue speaking, moving closer, breathing on him; "But I don't want to be groped in the office. Once might be considered an accident. Twice is definitely with intent. For the third time, I'd like a plan."

"Okay," Jeff is still smiling.

"And not in Ballybawn," I say.

"Okay," Jeff repeats.

"And soon."

"Okay."

Which is how we are lying sprawled across the sofa in town mouse's town pad. Or is that town mouse's mouse pad? I am not sure, but I am giggling again. Jeff is all sex and laughter. He touches my funny bones all over. Jumps my funny bones all over. Tickles my funny bones all over. We have just finished a marathon athletic sexual session since leaving Chez Jeffs in Dublin. Every part of my anatomy has been probed, assessed, stroked, caressed, rubbed and molested. At one stage I started to protest.

"I am not the vegetables, stop squeezing me!" But Jeff only smiled, his wolfish grin and squeezed harder.

There is something joyful in his exploration of my body. His pleasure in every protuberance and crevice is almost childlike.

"Oh, here we have a breast, lovely and wow, a taut nipple. Man, this is great. And look, there is a matching one. It feels just as good."

I am the main dish for his delight and boy does he delight.

It is four in the morning, and I am wide awake. I do not want to sleep. I want to play some more. Fortunately, so does Jeff. His capacity for sex is endless. Or is it just his wonder in the human form, the female form? Such endless joy and appreciation cannot be underestimated, undervalued or under-joyed.

Chapter Thirty-Three

Brigid is shocked. Of course, she doesn't show it quite like that, say it quite like that, but she means it just like that. She actually says very little and that I know is a bad sign. I have returned after 48 hours of love festing, love feasting, and I am glowing. Her view is that I have been sex festing, sex festering and it is showing.

"How does it show?" I want to ask her. "And why is it wrong?" Instead, I say nothing, see nothing, hear nothing.

We pass like ships in the night for days in a row. One arriving, one leaving. One staying in, the other going out. One on the telephone, the other silent. But the silence is not companionable. I am not sure how to fix it. I am not sure exactly where her disapproval lies. It is in the haste with which I slept with Jeff? Fuck, that's an oxymoronic statement if ever there was. Is it the haste with which I fucked Jeff? Possibly. Possibly so soon after Liam. But then sometimes to move on, one must replace. It is not enough to be. Or rather for me it is not enough just to be.

I am back working in the restaurant, but Miss Russian Coach is giving me jip. And lots of it. I am not sure this is going to work for much longer. Is Nicole the reason for Brigid's disapproval? I am not sure about that either. They are not married. Yes, they are going out in Ballybawn, but they appear not to be going out in Dublin city. Her stuff, that overused euphemism for things big and small, is not in his apartment. She is not in his apartment but I am.

"Semantics," Brigid says finally. We are sitting, unusually for us in this current hiatus, on the same sofa, in the same room, in the same house at the same time. Neither of us is leaving, going out or on the telephone. We just are. Moreover, the television is not on, and we are drinking a bottle of wine quickly. There is another at our feet, warm, red, and opened already. For this gathering we have to thank, or curse, Mick. He has deposited the wine and us in the same location. He has taken the dog into the kitchen and closed the door where he is smoking his foul cigars. He has said that we are to stay there and talk until one of us kills the other, or maims the other, or just bloody well talks to the other.

It turns out, after the first bottle of wine has been upturned and emptied, that we are not fighting at all. That first bottle of wine, warm and sweetly bloodish, flows down our throats barely touching the sides. Each grasps the wine glass as though it were a goblet, full handed. Sometimes both handed. Images of Elizabethan television drama bounce round my head as we swig great mouthfuls of the dark red juice and it slides down our throats, loosening our vocal chords, our mouths, our emotions.

My sleeping, that stupid, unrepresentative verb again, with Jeff while he is also dating Nicole is at the core of Brigid's unease. I look her in the eye. I want to tell her I don't give a flying fuck but that is clearly inappropriate. I want to tell her that Jeff is not tied to any one woman, not Nicole and certainly not me, but this is also totally irrelevant. I try to explain.

"Jeff is a man," I say.

Brigid's eyebrows plunge downwards unhelpfully.

I am not making a good job of this right now. "Jeff is a man who is also an artist," I say next. Eyebrows plunge further. This is obviously not a good tack to take.

"I am a woman," I begin.

This is even worse. But is it so bad that Brigid starts to smile.

"You are a fucking idiot!" she shouts. And then she laughs.

"I know, I know but it's great fun." I howl back in laughter, and I add quickly, "You cursed. You cursed so you must understand." And I am keen to make multiple points, to recover ground. But I have moved too quickly. Too suddenly. Too vaingloriously. The light in Brigid's eyes dies. She is suddenly sober. Oh fuck.

"I am your friend Bella," she says slowly. "I am always your friend. But I think this affair or bonkfest or whatever it is, is not a good idea. Not while you are living in Ballybawn with your husband stalking you, your mother stalking you and you stalking your ex-lover. It is just too much."

"I think you should move to Dublin. Carry on with Jeff or not but get the hell out of this goldfish bowl."

"What about George?" I ask.

"Just don't bonk him," advises Brigid sagely. "That's one complication too many."

Mick walks in on this last piece of advice. So does George. As if he has heard the advice, George, not Mick that is, jumps on Brigid, of whom he is very fond.

"I may leave him to you Brigid," I say as George's tail wagging sends him into sonic space. The empty bottle of wine is knocked over, which no one minds; the second bottle is almost similarly dispatched, which raises universal disapproval amongst the humans, and Brigid is left to fend off the amorous and loving pup by herself.

"If that is what it takes," she groans under a waggle of doggy ardour.

"How will you take it?" I ask Jeff in the midst of doggy-sex ardour.

"Like this," gasps Jeff between thrusts.

"No, how will you take it when I move in with you," I extend my sentence to the end and he too extends and ends.

"If you wish, but it is not a statement or a step along the way," he says later. "I am content for you to be here but do not ask for more."

"Is there more?" I wonder out loud, almost wistfully, in curiosity; Pooh bear like.

"No." Like Rabbit, the matter is closed. Jeff had just better hope I don't stick in the entrance for days. I've certainly had my fill of both honey and condensed milk, and like Pooh I've skipped the bread for fear of being greedy. I don't fancy the enforced diet nor the fact that my legs may be used for tea towel holders. I laugh so hard, but Jeff has not read Winnie the Pooh, and I cannot explain it to him. He just thinks I am barmy. And maybe I am. But it's a good barmy, full of laughter and fun. This is a good place for me, for Bella, for now.

Chapter Thirty-Four

I ring Brent. On the pub landline. As I listen to it ring, I imagine the sound echoing round the back hall. It is always cold and draughty in the hall, no matter how warm the bar or the back sitting room. I used to joke that a murder had taken place there; a crime of passion in the last century, or some drunken squabble ending in knives drawn. Brent never liked my murder fantasy and so I would play it harder. Talk about it while serving. Point to the condensation on the wall and liken it to blood pooling in a viscous puddle, slowly and inexorably spreading further and further.

I am interrupted from my reverie by the sound of my mother's voice. Stupidly I'd forgotten she was there too. Like the ghost, she too is hovering in the hall. I want to ask her what she can see, what she can feel in the hall. Can she sense the presence? What did happen after all? I start to frame my ludicrous line of questioning.

"Are you cold Mother, there in the hall?" I begin. "You know, I've always felt there was something strange about the hall. Where you are now. Do you feel the cold?"

But Mother is on her own pathway, her own purpose, and is not to be deflected by my random and inconsequential opening. Hearing my voice, she girds her metaphorical loins and raises up. I hear this in her very intake of breath. The inhalation of air into her lungs sets the scene. Then as she exhales and speaks into the phone, her breath comes rushing down the phone to me. Not over the wires as I am wireless of course. But through the air like the Valkyries, coming to take me away, to take me home, to take me to eternal salvation.

"I am bringing Father Roche to see you on Saturday," she says. "He has agreed to mediate between you and Brent. And for that matter, between you and me. We will all be there at 12 o'clock."

Oh, the Valkyries are alive and well but wearing black frocks and carrying rosary beads. Or am I just mixing up my religions? Who gives a fuck?

"Not I," says Odin. "I take all who fall in battle. Valhalla is my reward for you. When you fall in battle, give me a call and I'll send in the team."

I don't want to fucking battle. I want to fucking fuck. I am going to a place where I can laugh and forget all the fuck fools in Ballybawn, priests et al. And anyway, who wants to borne aloft by a bunch of beautiful maidens when your limbs are half hacked off in battle, when your organs are spewed by the side and when your hair is having a bad day? Not me, that's for sure. I've done the battling bit and I'm tired of the gore, the guts and the emotion strewn across the playground like litter. I'm tired too of the flabby muscle that is my heart pumping away and pimping my body and scrimping my feelings and cramping my joy.

I can just see those tight arsed Valkyries tut-tutting over my broken body, with wounds that can only be seen from above.

"She should have taken better care of herself." Or "just look at those split ends, so messy you know." Or "she's full of holes you know, seeping like a muslin cloth." I gird my fucking loins and yes, I fucking go out to battle, but quietly. I don't want Odin to hear.

"That is well and good, Mother, but I am ringing tonight to say that I am going away for a bit. I am not sure for how long, but certainly a couple of weeks. So, call up all you like, get Father Roche to mediate all you like, but I won't be there."

"Impossible girl," Mother splutters. "I only have limited time, and you are running away again. Just when I need you. Just when I need you."

It does not work. This blatant attempt at emotional blackmail. I needed you Mother much more when I was a child. You were never there. Or if you were, you were no help to me at all. There and not there. Present and yet absent. In the moment and yet not of the moment. Like that song, with the man of the weedy and plaintive voice, you left me Mother, just when I needed you most.

I hang up politely. Respectfully, if such a thing is possible. Ending a conversation when the other party is not finished is by default an act of rudeness. Yet, I didn't mean to be rude. I had finished the conversation, and while I am saddened that my mother had not reached the same moment of completion that I had, there was nothing to be gained by extending the conversation to accommodate her lingering, decaying words. I was not going to listen to them anyway. They were useless, redundant, and quite beside the point.

I look at my handset thoughtfully. I have ended, for the moment, this particular battle. I know it is only temporary. I know I have to revisit it. I know it will not go away, like an enemy army waiting for battle to commence. But there is a time for everything. And right now, I have bought myself some time and some space. I nod to Odin.

"Send the Valkyries home for a bit," I say. "Treat them to a spa night, a girlie weekend away, a night on the town. Give them, and me, a break from battle. I don't want Valhalla; not yet."

He, and his consort of beautiful maidens, nod back. They take to the sky, wheeling round in a vast circle and ride on a wave to the end of the world, my world, to the beginning of their world, Valhalla. My battles are not over yet. Not by a long chalk. But it is good to have friends in high places – for that bad hair day when it comes.

Chapter Thirty-Five

I am seduced by my stomach; bedded by my belly. I have moved into Jeff's apartment in Dublin. It is not a statement, he echoes, and to be honest I don't care. He is not mine. He is not my man. Except for the moment and I have no jealous care over him. Right now, it is right for me. Outside restaurant service I get a lot of his attention, and it is fun. He beds me and then feeds me. We are so hungry for each other we tumble into bed, into the kitchen, into any room in the apartment and tear each other's clothes off. Once we have exhausted our first round of sex, and there are many more to come, then we might eat. Or rather Jeff returns with edibles to eat, titbits to taste, snacks to seize upon and devour. Tom Jones has nothing on us. We eat with abandon and shed our mess on the floor, on the sheets, strewn with our clothes. We are too busy beginning Round Two to care.

In the morning, I cannot lie in. I get up, don my rubber gloves and clean. Obsessively yes, but not under a cloud. It is a joy, and I am cleaning up not cleaning out.

There is a purity of spirit in our relationship; I can't explain it. We ask the other for nothing. We both give generously, but don't ask for return. There are no ties. I am a little worried that this state cannot continue, but right now it feels so good. I want to give and give and give to Jeff. But I don't want to own him. I don't understand my newfound altruism. I am so enjoying the moment. I feel free and light and fun and sexy and good, and I am laughing, laughing, laughing. Jeff is laughing too.

I bought him The House at Pooh Corner book, but he refuses to read it. I try to read it to him, but he keeps on grabbing me. The minute I sit up cross legged and prepare to get down and dirty with Pooh Bear, he grabs me. Reading Winnie the Pooh is like a GO sign, and he starts nibbling my ear and plunging his hand inside my bra and tweaking my nipple. Then, he pops my fastener and opens my bra, releasing my breasts for his review. He moves behind me and cups my breasts in his hands, jigging them up and down, while he kisses my neck. I am sorry AA Milne but even your greatest fan cannot be expected to read through such seduction.

Jeff, now that he has won, just laughs and wanders off. I am so turned on I jump him and pull him back to bed. The forgotten book lies on the bed until it falls through our repeated movements. I will find it tomorrow half under the bed, the spine twisted. But for now, I am grabbing Jeff and forcing him to finish our passion. I pin him down and he laughs, his great big sexy laugh. His hands go up and fondle my breasts, again. He rubs my nipples. Then, he moves his hands down to my waist, and I move on top of him. Once linked in union, he takes my hands in his and arches them out. We move together, our hands spread eagle and tangled in the air, in perfect symmetry until he comes, I come, we come, and collapse in a tangle on the bed.

Of course, Jeff in the boudoir, and Jeff in the restaurant are two very different people. I trust the former, but the latter is a hard person to like, admire, yes, but not trust. Get it wrong and that knife might just go flying past your ear, regardless of all the perfect jobs begun, done and flung before. And one day, it might not fly past the ear. That slippage, that rush past the ear might have been precipitant, but how much more of a reaction if the target is made. Blood spilt in a second and perhaps an ear lies on the floor in a vulgar Van Gough pastiche. Like those revolting pig ears for sale in pet shops. I for one refuse to buy them for George regardless of how much he would like them. I wonder at the abattoir and how they harvest the ears; much in the same way as they harvest the prime steak no doubt. What is the difference? And how did I wander from Jeff to sliced ears?

Today I saw a butterfly, dead, on the floor in the apartment.

"Flutterbyes," Brigid's school children call them. But this beautifully coloured butterfly would flutter no more. Butter no more. Fly no more. Butterfly, butterflown.

Jeff the lover, I would trust on a knife edge. But Jeff the chef could as easily flutter by, butter fly, mutter by, and catch a passing critic, or eat a dining critic, or pimp a critic. When I said he was artist I was not far wrong. To be fair, he is pretty artistic in the bedroom, or is that enthusiastic and laughterful? But while his art in lovemaking, sexmaking is effortless, artless, his skill in the kitchen is regal and particular. Or is it a question of audience, of scale? In the bedroom he only has one to impress. I am not even the audience as I am on stage too. In the restaurant he serves up love plates for one, but many are called to inspect the creation. It is an act of love that he can share with the world, via critics, customers and a wider public willing to be seduced by their stomachs. In the kitchen, I can not trust him. His love for his food, his art, overflows and outweighs any personal emotion or loyalty. He is artistic and vain in his food, in a way that he is not with his body and his lovemaking. Therefore, I am glad I have invested in his sex and not in his food.

Regardless, I still take risks. Despite my knowledge of Jeff, albeit at a most intimate and yet frivolous and superficial level, I work for him in Chez Jeffs in Dublin. In Ballybawn, I was in purchasing, in Dublin I am promoted to front of house. Jeff obviously thinks I am up for the job. I am confident too and not watching my back for flying knives or butterflowns. But it takes confidence to face my lover fully in the restaurant. Not least of which is the fact I want to touch him during service and that is not on, at all.

But these are challenges that are all joys. I am made up. I don't know myself. For once, I am truly happy in the moment. I exist. I am. Therefore, I fuck Jeff. Just kidding. Actually, no, not just kidding.

Chapter Thirty-Six

"You do read."

It is an accusation, not a question.

"Of course."

"Why deny it then? Why pretend you are a gormless dolt?" Jeff is laughing but he is serious too. I want to laugh as well but his seriousness washes over me. I have always concealed my reading. Why? I did not want anyone to take it away from me, yes. Or to tease me, for sure. Or ridicule me, definitely. My mother did not read. Except, predictably, the tea leaves and she was not very good at that. At least none of the pronouncements she made for herself ever seemed to come true. I did not drink tea on principle, even bags, for fear I might be read. It was the same with books, or rather I was never seen to read.

Instead, I read under covers, out of sight, in harmless silos where I could not be found. I was catholic in my reading; universal in my appetite. I would as soon read Mills & Boon as struggle through Desmond Morris. Actually, now that I think of it, I didn't struggle as much as devour Desmond Morris and his Naked Ape. I think that book, aged nine or so, first opened my eyes to the possibilities of what might lie in books. What information I might glean. Of course, it depended on the previous tenants where my reading went. Like an idle tourist in a local taxi, I ventured down lanes and up escarpments all at the whim of my drivers;

those that went before, those that were kind enough, bored enough to leave behind their books, dog eared, pawed and panted over. I must have read every romance ever written; and hated them all with a passion. I became a bit of a crime aficionado and could spot the murder weapon, motive and culprit a mile off. And I have read a million non-descript books that left me dry and gasping. Yet, there was never a book I would not finish. A bad habit I realise now, but one I cannot ignore. Once I open a book and read the opening pages, nothing short of total oblivion would stop me finishing the book. I may shout and yell and curse the whole way through as I hate, hate, hate the book, the plot, the author but I will finish the fucking thing. I will not let a book better me. By the same token—and that's not a book token—once I've taken against an author, I know better than to open another book by the same person. If I don't open it, I don't have to read it.

Jeff is still waiting for my answer. Patiently. We are having breakfast together; rolls and coffee continental style, Jeff style. He is reading the Irish Times, I am reading The House at Pooh Corner. Actually I am not reading the book, I am letting the familiar words enter my brain and rejoin the residual memory from when I last read the book and from the time before that and before that, ad finitum. There is no active role here, just the consensual yeses and nods as words are filtered through my brain to meet the memories of before.

"Well, do you write as well?," Jeff asks in some seriousness.

"I read," I agree, tardily but conscientiously answering his first question. "Compulsively. And without a shred of discernment. You name it, I read it. And typically forget it ten minutes later."

Most of the stuff I have read I cannot recall. Books are lodged in my brain like shards of glass, small reflections of the sum filtered by time, energy, and place. Some books host sway where they were read in good times or have energies of their own or pinpointed an emotion I was experiencing at the time. Last month, I read McEwan's Atonement and cried throughout the denouement. I wanted to rewrite my brief history. But then here I am in Jeff's, and the book has lost its coveted place. Reranked downwards in a progressive twist of fate; the book has not changed but I have.

"I don't write," I say. "What would I write?"

The only book I have kept with me is AA Milne's. I read it as a child in wonder. I reread it as a teenager in boredom probably, but I've returned to it as an adult in wonder again. It was the one book I owned. Mother did not give it to me, and she hated it. I found it on more than one occasion in the bin. But it was mine and I clung to it stubbornly. Eventually, I threw it away myself when I married Brent. Or rather, I put it away. The time was then; a time to put away childish things and become a woman. A woman married. A time to cleave to my husband. I did not throw it in the bin, but I left it in my flat for the next tenant to read. The next rental tourist who might put out their hand and read about the bear of little brain. And as I was putting things childish from me, so too was Brent. Only mine was a book, and his was his sister. There was nothing childish in their encounter. A bear of very little brain - yet still, he might capture a heffalump. What had I caught?

"Write? Are you mad?" I answer Jeff in the present. The past is swirling around my brain today and I cannot rewrite it, re-right it. Fuck off McKwan for giving me a glimpse of paradise postponed and rejoined, again. Giving me hope for making the wrong right, writing the wrong right.

"Karleen wants to talk to you about writing. Expressing she called it," Jeff says. And at his comment, I am whirled back to the previous Saturday. Karleen is the editor of True You, a tabloid glossy women's monthly. The usual mix of celebrity, fashion, and diet. Jeff and I, almost as a couple, joined Karleen and her graphics designer, after their meal, after service, after hours. I talked the hind legs off the fucking donkey. I was in flying form, without a knife to be seen. Eeyore would have been proud of me.

"Ring her," commands Jeff.

"Don't mind if I do," I retort.

Chapter Thirty-Seven

Karleen's offices are bright. A wall of windows lines one side of her office, and the late morning sunlight streams in. Along the far wall are stacked hundreds of magazines. Piled high in paper mountains, thousands of words all resting quietly together, jostling slightly for space. On the wall are the framed front covers, twelve in total, one for each edition of the magazine from last year.

"If a magazine can survive a year, then it can survive forever," Karleen says following my gaze.

"I stopped framing the covers once I got to twelve. True You has cracked the market. We're a name, a brand, a must buy for young Irish women. But I can't ever rest. We are literally only as good as the last edition. If we slow up or lose the pace, then we lose the reader, the purchaser."

"Only ever as good as our last edition," she repeats looking at me. "Which is where you come in."

I shift in my chair. When I phoned last night and was subsequently summoned to Karleen's offices, I was not really sure why I was here. I ask Karleen this question. "Why am I here?"

"I liked what you said the other night. It was funny. It was sharp. It was totally irreverent. You had something to say on every topic; not necessarily opinions that I would share, but opinions that were lively and, well, opinionated! I'd like to feature some of your thoughts in the magazine. A kind of angry young woman column." Karleen sits back as she says this and joins the tips of her fingers together. She pats them softly and smiles. "What do you think? Are you up for it?"

"I can't write," I say.

"Doesn't matter," Karleen retorts. "I'll have it subbed in here. It's your opinions, your rants that I want rather than your style that I want. Just tell it like it is."

I think for a moment. There is no downside to this. Either it works or it doesn't. I get paid if it works. If it doesn't then I don't, and I have not lost anything in the process. And it would be fun I reckon.

It is agreed and we do lunch. I have never done lunch before. It is on expenses. I like this. "Do I get expenses?" I ask. "If the column works," is the answer. I decide over a fucking nice lunch with margaritas to begin, and lots of Chablis to wash down our salads, that I am going to make this column work. But next time I'm having the steak.

Later as I sit in front of the flickering laptop screen, I am very bad - tempered. Whose fucking idea was this? What possessed me to think that I could write or even have an opinion? I am totally bereft of ideas. What do I want to opine on? Fuck knows. Who would want to fucking read what I write, if I could fucking write in the first place.

I leave the torture seat and walk to the kitchen. Why am I here? I open cupboards erratically. Pull out contents and read the labels. I open the fridge door and see an open bottle of wine, with a stopper in it. I pour myself a glass and rest against the large American fridge. The ice maker cackles into the life and fresh cubes are flipped over into the icebox ready for immediate dispensing.

I swirl the wine round in my glass. It frosts the sides. I keep on telling Jeff that the fridge is too cold but he doesn't listen. The fridge is very much his domain. I might clean it but I don't order it, order him.

I watch the condensation climb the edges of the glass, pull up the sides and then retreat like waves on the beach. Angrily, I down the wine in one swallow and feel the cold liquid flood my insides.

I am now angry at Jeff, at Karleen, at my own stupidity, that I might be able to write anything of interest. I wander back to the living room. The TV is on in the corner, but I turn it off and turn on the stereo. Jeff's taste is music is excruciating fuck awful. I don't like Phil Collins, ever. Or George Michael. And I never liked Queen. Or maybe I am just the wrong generation. Who knows, but I hate everything in the CD stand. I turn back on the TV. I turn on the music channels but there is nothing I want to watch. I flick from channel to channel. I am totally wrecked. I cannot sit still, cannot watch television, cannot write a single word, cannot listen to any music. I need out.

And so, I find myself walking the streets, pounding the pavements, hands stuffed in my pockets and head tucked into my hoodie. I walk and I walk and I walk. Then I begin talking to myself. Not out loud, -or rather only some words,- but mostly under my breath, as I swear, and curse and laugh. I am not sure what is going on, but I am just restless, nervous, shaky, interested, blocked, doubting and confident - all at the same fucking time. I wonder if I am coming down, or missing Tony from Ballybawn. There is, of course, plenty of coke in Dublin, but I don't have a regular source, and Jeff just doesn't, so I don't around him.

I turn for home and as I do a familiar figure looms in front of me.

"Bella, what is the matter?" And it is Jeff. I laugh.

"Writer's block," I shout at him. I pull at his arm and wheel round and round him. He is strong and pulls me into him, forcing me to stop turning.

"I am stronger than I look," he said once, as he carried me, still impaled, from the kitchen counter to the dining room table which was a better height. I wonder who he seats at that spot during dinner parties. He has not hosted any since I have been there, so I have yet to find out if it is the place of honour or insult.

"Why don't you write about things you know about," he says, pulling me tighter yet. He is talking into my ear and then kissing it, and then my neck. He pulls me closer yet and moves his mouth to mine. We are kissing on the street and moving together in unison, pulsating in a slow pleasurable fashion. His tongue laps mine and he sucks my mouth, pulling me in. It is a long-time kissing, like teenagers do, but without the excess saliva. It is a time of the soul. The kiss refreshes those parts that the beer cannot meet. Then it hits me. Sex. I shall write about sex. Easy peasy lemon squeezy.

Chapter Thirty-Eight

Sex. Oh, yes, that was an easy decision to make. Now I have to fulfill my own self-promise. It is four o'clock in the morning. Jeff is asleep, breathing quietly, with his arm thrown back across his head. The pose is very childish and dreamlike, and quite unlike the forceful man who took me earlier. I am sore and bruised and pierced, like a ripe peach that has been squeezed firmly by its owner, rolled between his palms, and then bitten suddenly, sharply, with hunger.

The laptop is perched on the side of the bed. My bedside lamp is on and its low light pools around me, giving a poker-like atmosphere to the room. I am hunched over the keyboard and its flickering screen. I am reminded of a Peanuts cartoon in which Snoopy is writing his novel on top of his kennel. 'It was a dark and stormy night' was his opening and only line. He sits there, upright in front of his typewriter, and types and retypes those frozen words, never progressing, never telling any more. As a child, I wanted to know more. I could not understand his dilemma. Words poured out of me like water rushing from a tap; I just never spoke them aloud. I never took breath, I never slowed up.

They just tumbled, rushed, splashed out in total disarray, and without much sense of order or sense. Joyous is a good word to describe my verbal diarrhoea. But nobody ever heard it because I never spoke it aloud. I walked in a cloud of words, ideas and thoughts. By day, a dysfunctional, awkward, monosyllabic child of an alcoholic, by parallel day a child oozing words. Puffing them out like smoke every time I opened my mouth. Great big steaming clouds of words, popping soundlessly in the air.

What would set me off? Some idle word, read, heard or overheard. Crate of olives, barrel of laughs, salted herrings, sitting on the dock of the bay. I cannot remember but it happens even now. I start with one little word and before I know it, I have planted a forest, a veritable jungle in my mind.   It's fucking great.

But now, in the puddled light, I am dismayed to find I am even behind Snoopy in literary achievements. Paper might never have refused ink, but a flickering screen can sure repel words.

Jeff finds me in the morning sprawled across the bed with the laptop still turned on. He has read the screen and is laughing softly.

"I don't think Karleen wanted you to write porn," he says. "Write about sex by all means, but write about the variety, the issues, the dilemmas, the differences, the sameness, the quirky ones, the straight ones, but don't write explicit sex scenes. Apart from anything else, I don't want to read about our sex in your column. Unless, of course, it is brilliant!"

"It's always fucking brilliant," I lie, but then I think for a moment and actually that's not a lie. So far, anyway. Can good sex last beyond six weeks, six months, six years, I wonder. I mean really good, to die for sex? At what point does the urge falter and fade, when does the penis lie flaccid and untouched for days on end, when does the urge to bump and grind seep through the gravel and disappear like sudden rain on a hot day. Was it ever there? And what can we compare it to? Former lovers, girlfriend confidences, erotica, films, reality television? And why do some of the most repellent, fuck ugly people seem to have the hottest sex? Do they try the hardest?

I submit a short rant on why ugly people have the best sex and also, my pornographic semi-autobiographical description of our sex the night before. Funnily enough, Karleen takes both. Two for the price of one springs to mind as she only pays one commission. Jeff is not overjoyed. He is not joyous. He is very pissed off that I submitted the explicit porn scene as well.

"Look," he says, almost spitting in anger. "If I lick your pussy, that is good, but not when the world can read about it. I don't want our sex to go under the microscope of Dublin critics. Apart from anything else, if it gets out that you are shagging me, then I will be literally fucked." He draws breath. "And when things go wrong are you going to write about our shite sex? How I can't get it up or I come too soon, or you don't feel like it but blame me for the lack of arousal. I'm not fucking having it."

But I am concentrating on his earlier statement. "What do you mean that if it gets out, I am shagging you that you will be literally fucked," I ask. "What does that mean?"

Jeff pauses mid diatribe. He has the good grace to look ashamed. Only I don't give him any credit whatsoever for he replies: "My wife will take me to the cleaners."

Now I am confused.

Chapter Thirty-Nine

"How can a celebrity, even a minor one like Jeff, have a wife that no one knows about?" asks Brigid in disbelief.

We are sitting on the dock of the bay, watching the tide roll away. We are sitting on the frayed yellow sofa, watching the dog fart away. We are both drinking wine, and wasting our time, but we're in no hurry and there is plenty of it -and plenty of wine and even plenty of foul smells from George.

I am enjoying playing the master of ceremonies, unveiling the truth in the slowest way possible. I began right at the very beginning and am now only midway. But with Brigid's eyebrows rising steadily, I don't know if I can hold out much longer.

"America," I say finally. "It was a teenage holiday romance. Summers spent in Cape Cod. Aged nineteen, she, Carol, got pregnant. They have a son with a severe mental handicap. Problems during birth, lack of oxygen to the brain. But then Carol told no one and had their child, Jerome, in her sister's bedsit. The emergency services were only called when Carol's sister returned home unexpectedly from work and found Carol hemorrhaging in the bathroom."

Brigid is aghast and puzzled in equal parts.

"But, rich kids in Cape Cod don't have babies in bedsits," she says.

And I deliver the final piece of the jigsaw. "Carol is black."

The picture is now complete and not necessarily that pleasant. Jeff, spoilt Irish rich kid, spends summers in Cape Cod with surgeon father and socialite mother. Falls for Carol in teenage romance. Leaves for college back in Ireland after a summer of illicit sex with Carol. Carol falls pregnant. And here I pause. How do women fall pregnant? The image is vivid. I see rows of women, young, old, fat, skinny, tall, short, all falling like dominos, one after the other, falling on to one another in a cascading puddle of women. And when they fall, they have bellies vast as melons. Taut as footballs. They fall on their sides, bellies forward, outward, falling into motherhood.

Carol, poor as a church mouse, daughter of a cleaner for one of those so American country clubs, where golf, tennis, teenage discos and grown-up swinging, well I imagine the swinging, but certainly drinking and flirting amongst the bony, tanned women and expansive men. Leaning into conversations, oh so witty, haw haw haw, peering down cleavages, patting rumps on the way to the bathroom and all-round bonhomie. Fuck off you bastards. There is Carol. Shagged by Jeff in a frantic bid for independence.

"Fuck off Mummy," he says as he plunges his shaft into her. The strangeness of her, her skin, her breasts, her clawing at him when she comes, crying into his mouth. He is declaring war. He is conquering hero. He is cutting through the racial crap and prejudice. He is striking a blow for racial freedom with every thrust. Racial. Freedom. Pant. Pant. This is the way the world ends, not with a whimper but a bang.

Only his world doesn't end. His bid for freedom, for independence, for justice, for fuck you mother, ends in him going back to college.

For Carol, the ending is very different. Seven months later, she is bleeding in her sister's bedsit. Only her sister, nameless, has forgotten her cigarettes, and returns to red blood, and lots of it, and a child struggling to claim his first breath, to tell Jeff that his bid for independence, for freedom, is over.

"Here I am, Dad," calls Jerome. He pants too, but it is not orgasm he seeks but life. Liquid is in his lungs, and he puffs and sucks and pants and cries and shrieks and pulls onto life.

"I choose life," he says. Carol lies on the floor, incapable of choosing now. Unnamed sister calls emergency services. Does she cradle Carol's head? Does she peer between Carol's legs? Does she light a cigarette? I don't know. Jerome might know if he had sense now.

"I saw a light," Jerome might have said, might yet say. He is seventeen now. Wheelchair bound. He looks like Jeff, a black version of Jeff. Without the motor skills, without the verbal skills, without the mental skills. Whom, as Lucy or Linus or perhaps it was Peppermint Patty said, whom are we fucking kidding? Only his light was into the world and not out of it. Poor fucker, he wasn't even given a choice. Nameless sister intervened and Carol ended up in hospital, and they finally extracted Jerome, senseless and stupid.

There is no nice ending to this story. Just because Carol was black and poor does not mean she wanted a disabled child and would love him. Just because Jeff wanted to fuck his mother and kill his father and strike a blow for freedom, does not mean that he wanted Jerome either. His idealism, in fairness to Jeff, led him, after his parents attempted a clumsy payoff, to fly back to the States and marry Carol.

The awkward ceremony, no relatives because all were feuding, one side wanting to be shot of the other, the other wanting recompense, was beyond awful. Carol, for all that she was black, could be described as pale, bleached, wan, it was not enough, their love child had screamed on the way out, let me out, let me out, and they had failed him together. Jerome was love child. Terribly wounded and forever sealed in his airtight drum. Lack of oxygen had damaged him beyond awful.

Oedipus might have smiled that day. He might have fucked off and gone out for a beer with Odin. They can see backwards and forwards, can't they? Into the past and into the future. But Oedipus had feet of clay, swollen feet from when he hung from the tree. Lack of oxygen probably screwed his brain as a child when he swung upside down from the tree, swung and waited for a peasant to rescue him, and put his swollen feet back upon the path. Did he know then what he would do or was it only in hindsight his knowledge came. Isn't it seductive when mere mortals follow your lead, oh you gods? Except poor Jeff didn't fuck his mother, didn't kill his father and has a severely damaged son with a severely disaffected wife. There is no happy ending here.

I, for whom unhappiness is second nature, feel sorry for Jeff. But it is not a good place for me to be. Jeff is my running-away-place, my sex-playground, my oh-my-god place. I don't want him to have soft, moist, vulnerable chunks of rotting flesh. He has to be impermeable, rock hard, invincible. He can be eclectic, winsome, actually not winsome, but humoursome maybe. Brigid thinks I am shallow. And I agree.

Chapter Forty

We are all damaged. All lacking. There is no holistic being, even in Christ, maybe especially not in Christ. His wounds are pierced in his side and flowing with blood. His hands, the stigmata, through which blow vast tracts of doctrine, tumbleweed in the desert, tumbleweed at the foot of his cross where vinegar was the only solace, screaming into his wounds, into his thirst, quenching nothing.

We might arrive without sin on conveyor belts from heaven. Little cherubs with fat cheeks and dimpled asses, but with the first crap we are polluting the world. Poor Jerome didn't even have the conveyor belt treatment. He was held back by the stiff plastic doors that block the luggage from the carousel. I see him now, swimming frantically towards the doors, pushing, battering, beating tiny fists against the tough, dirty see-through flaps. Was it harder, I wonder, to see the arrivals hall but not be able to gain it?

Sympathy is not my thing, but I feel for the whole fucking lot of them. What a fucking mess.

Brigid is shaking her head too. There is no sense to the story. Now, Carol is a hairdresser, a step up from cleaner's daughter, but she has a drink problem, like her mother before her. Jerome has 24x7 care, paid for by Jeff but is without his father. Carol is a mess. Jeff is absent. Jerome is stuck in that fatal moment of birth, gasping, always gasping for his share of oxygen. But that is the limit for my sympathy.

"We all get dealt a hand of cards," I say. Meaning is lost through wine, or is it gained? Either way, rhetoric is false right now. Dripping with false truth. "It's how you play them," I finish off lamely.

Brigid looks at me.

"Some cannot play them at all," she says. "There is no choice, just survival. And survival can be just as important."

But, if it were my time to be story master at first, now it is Brigid's. She has waited patiently, and it must be said with interest, to my story, or rather Jeff's story, or is it Jerome's, or even Carol's? It is a collective story of waste, of burden, of beginnings begun badly and ending just as terribly. There is no real joy to be found, no spirit lifting finale that makes us glad. Only harsh reality that drags us down. I am drained by the end.

Before we leave this first empty sounding gong, before we can move to Brigid's bright new tale, she wants to know why, what Carol can do to my column, what would she do to it, why would she know of my story of lust with Jeff? It is simple enough, I explain. He has not divorced her, again the idealist, tempered by age and pocket, but he does nothing to attract her umbrage when it comes to women. By going public with my sex column or my semi-autobiographical pornographic tales, I might expose him, or at the very least create a problem. I think I have it sorted though as Karleen is not using my name.

Nor have I written faux commentary such as "Ireland's keenest sushi chef swapped the taste of organic sea farmed fish for his lover's pussy". Call me old fashioned, but I have my fucking standards.

But onto Brigid's tale, which is wetted and waiting and wanting for me. Conrad George Creighton. She has found an address that she thinks might be his. She even rang up to check the number, but was too worried to bluff it out properly. She pretended calm and asked if 'Conrad George Creighton' was at this number. The woman who answered said yes, but who was calling. Brigid faltered at this point and flustered and basically hung up.

"But I have an address," she said triumphantly, pushing a piece of paper into my hand.

I look at the address. Ballsbridge in Dublin. A very fucking posh address. Maybe he is loaded? He'd have to be loaded at this address.

"Unless he is living in the doorway," I laugh at Brigid.

"Homeless in Ballsbridge." She laughs too but is eager to accept the paper, the news, the possibility.

I look at the address again and wonder at a different past. Maybe a different present. I see, for the fleetest moment, Daddy buying me floaty dresses and spinning me round and round in his arms. His little princess, he says as he smiles indulgently, eyes twinkling at me. It is a fucking crock of shite. The fleetest moment is about five seconds long. What a fucking waste of a fucking father. Even in my aspiration moments, my daydreams, of which there are very little I have to say, very fucking little, he doesn't last longer than five seconds. No wonder my fucking relationship with men is so fucked up, so fleeting, so flawed.

I am stunned by my reaction to the address. Once that fucking fleeting thought evaporates, I am so fuck angry. Brigid blinks at my anger, which rushes out of me like a flood, a deluge of red hot emotion. She physically backs off as though I have threatened to hit her. I am raised up, like a cobra, ready to strike. But strike what? It is only a piece of paper in my hand.

A piece of paper in my hand. This piece of paper in my hand. I uncoil my body. I reject the adrenaline coursing through my veins. I breathe slowly. I put aside the imaginations of daddyhood. Actually, I feck them off to the farthest point of my brain, to the very litter scum hole where no one goes. Not even me. And not my fucking father.

Chapter Forty-One

I am tumbled out of a dream. The edges are all grainy, muted into sepia. I am walking, no, running, always running, but I am running into terror. This really upsets me. Why can't I run away? Why am I running towards that which frightens the fuck out of me? And it is worse because I do not know what it is I fear.

Once, I had a recurring dream. I was trapped in a tall tower, a skyscraper, a hotel, and it was on fire. I was trying to rescue another child, how connected to me I don't know, I just knew I was responsible, whether sibling or friend or just child, it was never clear to me. The dream persisted over a period of about two years, beginning around the time I was with Brent. Each time I entered the dream it was with a familiar terror. Each time was slightly different, but I would look out a window, far up in the sky, smell the smoke, and then look back into the hotel room and hear the child crying. I would dream this nightmare every three months or so. It became so bad, I stopped sleeping. I would drink until I was very drunk, pouring more spirits down my throat even when I was full, full to overflowing. I wanted to go to bed and not dream.

The horror was when I did sleep and still entered the dream. That window in the sky was enough to send me into sweats. It meant I would not use lifts anymore, would not enter a building that was more than four storeys, and I could not use the stairs.

Then I had a brainwave. An attack of genius. I woke one night still drenched from the dream. I cannot even begin to detail the anguish, the fear, the absolute terror. I cannot detail it because to detail it would make it real. I woke, terrified, unsuccessful in my bid to rescue the crying child. Unsuccessful in my bid to rescue me. Perishing in the blinding smoke and the terror and the sheer futility of striving, surviving. . As I lay there, drenched in sweat and panting, I realised the problem lay in the physical, which is slightly weird because we are talking about a dream, albeit recurring so that it takes on a more permanent focus. But the physical problem with the dream lay in the height of the building, and the problem that when I looked out the window, I was up at the uppermost levels, and the fire was already rife.

If a fire broke out in a hotel and I was on the ground floor, then how much more likely would I be to escape? And perhaps the crying child might not be mine, or rather not my responsibility anymore, and even if still my responsibility, then at least we might be both on the ground floor. Drenched in sweat as I was and still slipping out of my sleep, I re-entered the dream. It was not that difficult, the sweat on my chest was still hot, and I was balanced between the world of sleep and waking. I closed my eyelids, flattened them against eyeballs. Saw the images close up, closer than normal as I faced them, and forced an image of a reception desk and made the booking for a ground floor room. As I surfaced, I felt something like regret. But after two years of dread, I never dreamt that dream again. Losing the dream was like losing an old friend, but one that I had grown tired of and could not ditch. I am not sentimental, but its loss was felt, welcomed but noted too.

Dreams and reality. How closely are they bound? Did Maria have a recurring dream before she fell? Did she walk to the edge in her dreams, in her sleep, her eyelids flickering rapidly? Falling in dreams can last forever. In dreams, the shuddering stop thud is never there, never felt, the never end is never there. There is only the rush, the whoosh, the speed, the journey, Alice floating down the tunnel.   Nowhere is the bone breaking, flesh pulverising, sickening end to life. Bones, tissue, muscle, organs all mulched up in a single violent blow. Swat, the fly is dead. Thud, the body breaks apart. In a moment. Life: then whoosh, not life.

Chapter Forty-Two

There is no talking to Mother. I tell Brigid again. But Brigid is not listening to me, or rather she is listening to me, but taking absolutely no notice of what I say.

"Talk to your mother first." She repeats obstinately.

I cannot fight her. Even George is giving me the eye. Mick has been in and murmured something about good starting points. I am totally fucked up, fucked out and plain fucked off. There is also the question of Brent. Call me a fucking ostrich but I just don't want to see him. I want to bury my head in the sand. I want to ignore him totally. I just don't want the agro.

Which is why I am fucking walking over to the pub in the foulest mood ever to descend on Ballybawn, to face the two people I least want to see in the world. I have left George behind, but he is quite happy with Brigid. If it weren't for Mick I might spread some inter-genus rumours. I still might.

Brent is serving. I sit up at the bar and order a pint.

"You're home," he says curtly.

"No, I'm visiting. My home is no longer here."

He looks at me and through me. I see his anger rising like waves up and across his face, pulling red in its wake. There are three other people in the pub, all regulars and all listening with alacrity. A pin could drop and it would be heard. I fantasise with the notion of testing this theory, of asking Brent for the loan of a pin. A smile must have flickered across my face because his face tightens even closer. His lips are practically pursed. It is not a good look. I want to ask him to relax, to let his face relax, but it does not matter. How he looks is no concern of mine anymore.

"Is Mother still here?" I ask instead.

"What do you think?"

I actually think that it's fucking weird that my mother is still here. Why isn't she dead yet? Or sick even? And why the fuck is Brent allowing her to stay? How on earth do they manage to co habituate? Is it some self-inflicted punishment that Brent has decided to undergo? And if so, for what purpose? It's not bringing me back and it's sure as fuck not bringing Maria back.

As if on cue, my mother emerges from the back lounge. She looks alive. She is moving. Her legs take one step after another, and she moves towards me. She is ambulatory. She is speaking. To me. I watch her approach. I watch her lips and the words issuing. It is all the mediation crap stuff still. I hear snippets between her breaths, priest this, talk that, return this etcetera, etcetera.

"How are you Mother? How is the cancer?" I ask and that stops her fast. Mid-sentence even. She splutters, retreats a little. No one is obviously asking her about her cancer despite or because of her great denouement when she first arrived. There is only so much bad news we can all take. Only so much cancer we can tolerate, even at a harmless remove.

"Not great," she says, spreading her hands out in supplication, palms up, "But I am surviving," she adds.

"Good, then you can tell me about Conrad George Creigton."

If my asking after her cancer stopped her before, this has the effect of totally freezing her. Her face falls, frozen, into a grimace. Her hands flop from supplication to limp and then to fists, in a moment, hardening, freezing into balls of fingered ice.

She is rigid and still. Even her breathing is suspended. Finally, she speaks, and the words jerk out of her like rusty nails prised from a worn sleeper.

"You have been through my possessions, Looking at my things." Ping, ping, ping.

"Actually, Mother, technically my birth certificate is my possession, not yours. Ping, fucking ping, right back at you.

Chapter Forty-Three (or possibly earlier) 1985

Afternoon tea in the Shelbourne. An ornamental cake stand. Filled with scones, butterfly cakes, tea cakes, marble cake slices. The tea is served in a silver pot, made with real leaves, and poured through a silver strainer. The china is bone and patterned. Her hands shake a little as she pours the tea. She has forgotten to add the milk first. She smiles nervously, looking up from under long lashes, like Lauren Bacall, or so she hopes. He smiles indulgently, a slight paunch already present under his shirt, pressing up to the edge of his belt and pushing over slightly.

He takes the cup and saucer from her trembling hands. The china rattles imperiously, cup against saucer and mindless of the handler. He places two lumps of brown, crystallized sugar into the black tea, adds a generous portion of milk, and stirs it vigorously, knocking the ornate teaspoon against the edges, clink, clink, clink, round it goes.

When he drinks, it is with a great big slurp, fleshy lips engulf the smooth china, and the tea rushes towards his mouth. His head rocks backwards and in three mighty swallows the tea is gone. The cup looks diminutive in his large hands, saucer held primly in one, pinky extended in the other.

She rubs her nose with her right hand, index and middle finger scratching an imaginary itch. Next, she smoothes her cheek bone, tracing her fingers along the skin to her hairline before trailing down to her jaw and dropping back into her lap. Her tea is poured but untouched in front of her.

Her knees are tightly bunched together. Pressing hard so that there is a large red mark on each inner knee, the mark is still there when she visits the bathroom later. The heat in the hotel's tearooms is on high. Her thighs are perspiring slightly. She wishes to air them but dare not release her knees. Who knows who might fly in?

Chapter Forty-Four (or possibly earlier)

He has borrowed the car, a vast Mercedes of indeterminate age, from his uncle. She shrinks back from him in the leather interior. It is too big, too grand for their jaunt. She is wearing jeans but wishes she had put on a skirt. The leather is too squeaky for denim. She feels under-dressed, although they are only travelling to Dun Laoghaire to walk on the pier.

He parks it awkwardly but with bluster. She is too timid, too awed to comment. Driving it strikes her as a feat in itself, parking it only serves to confirm her amazement. She does not drive. Has only travelled on her brother's motorbike, badly, upright and rigid, and does not understand mechanical things.

Her mode of transport is the public bus, pushbike, or Shank's mare. The bus is not real to her. The driver is not real. It is a thing that comes, picks up passengers, and spits them out. She does not see the driver -or their skill, or lack thereof. She sits quietly on the bus, smoking upstairs, and watches out the condensation covered windows-always condensation, regardless of the weather.

The push bike is just so damn hard. Everywhere is uphill, even the downhill. Nothing can be carried with ease, and only the most repellent of shoes will survive the pedals. And when it rains -, well don't even go there.

Today, she is on Shank's mare. Not the normal Shanks's mare—even she would agree—but she's too awed to contemplate what level of mare she's riding. And would the audience down the back please behave. Stop making lewd comments at this point. There is nothing gross or indecent about her behaviour. All is purity and panting and light. So carry on drinking your cider or beer if you must, but leave the poor girl alone. She is on a date. In a big merc. With a man she admires, and perhaps even fancies. Any reference to riding is purely coincidental, and you can keep your dirty thoughts to yourself thank you very much.

He locks the doors with a great effort of effortlessness. If she were less impressed, she might have noticed that great show of devil - may - care is in direct contrast to his clumsy parking. Even now, after several reversals and stallings, the car is crossing badly into the next space. It is sure to make anyone wishing to park on the right hand side very pissed off indeed.

He extends his hand and gathers her little fist into his great maw. They set off to promenade. This is what couples do on a weekend. She is not sure they are a couple yet. They have kissed, it must be admitted, calm down you lousy crew at the back, we are talking demure here. They have been on several, shall we call them outings? Dates? It is so hard to tell in the 80s. They are on the verge of being a couple. The only thing holding them back is sex. And why is that holding them back? This is the fucking 80s, for fucks sake? It may have something to do with the fact that she is only fourteen.

Chapter Forty-Five (or possibly earlier)

Shopgirl and student. She doesn't really attend school anymore. She is present in the flesh - but not attending, not attentive, not achieving. She works in a late-night corner shop after school, and this is where she is alive. School with its algebra, battles and verbs is totally incomprehensible to her. Life in the minimart is infinitely more real. She is not stupid, but just not interested in the conundrums posed by the teachers. Or the stupid control devices employed by them. She blanks over, freezes over, zones out.

At work, while not exactly the scintillating experience perhaps promised by television or the films - at least provides daily interest and human shite. Well, not literally shite you, pissed crew at the back. Just the flotsam and jetsam of humanity being squeezed through the late opening doors of this minimart, collecting tampons, milk, dog food, bread, the necessities of life when they are needed. Shop in a supermarket and you shop for the week. Shop in a late-night minimart and you shop for the emergency and include wine and beer in that equation. But fuck, that loud crew down the back.

"You've had enough, do you hear? Fuck off to the chippie and sober up before you come back to heckle here. Or just plain fuck off. You didn't make it the first time round and you are surely not going to make it in the retelling."

Chapter Forty-Six (or possibly earlier)

An inland girl, water and the sea makes her nervous. Rivers, streams, even lakes, she can understand, but the tide makes her restless. It makes her twitch and rap her fingers in a loosely rhythmical roll. Rat a tat, a tat. Instead of the distant rumble easing her, it pushes her to alertness. It is the beat of the jungle that precedes a battle, the roar of the enemy in preparation for fight.

> This is an ordeal, not an experience. She is not sure if he will hold her hand or expect her to stride confidently - out in front, beside or perhaps even loll slightly behind. There is water, and waves crashing on both sides of her and she is unnerved.

They walk, bumping into each other, because he, for all his air of confidence, is living on bravado. Hands are finally captured again, and they walk swinging, but it is not an easy alliance.

> She looks at his hand, her hand in his. He has dressed with his usual care, in his usual uniform, shirt and jumper, elbow-patched tweed jacket, scarf tied against the cold today but normally worn regardless of heat. His arms are too long for his jacket sleeves or are they too wide? It is hard to decide but the end result is awkward or perhaps childish, arms sticking out of sleeves. What marks the child from the man are the hairs, thousands of them, long and dark red, bristling along the backs of his wrist. His beard, if let grow, is also

reddish. He prefers a smooth finish, so she does not know this, nor will she know this, not until she gives birth and the early morning shadow flashes red brown before it, he, scarpers for good.

Strawberry blonde is his hair. She sings this in her mind before sleep. It is his crowning glory, his pièce de résistance. She has not seen him naked - yet and will never see him naked. All his wonder is captured in his hair, haloed and curled around his face. The strange corpulence of him is shrouded and secret. It repels and excites her in equal parts, but her romance is buried in his hair and his face, his eyes. So too in his fingers, large but tender and soft. He brushes her cheek and electricity flashes along her skin.

There is no me, no I in this story, not yet. Hush, you 'wanna - be's. I was chosen, not you. I am still waiting in the wings. And so, I see the beauty in the story - the frailty, the utter futility, fuck me. fuck her. fuck me.

Chapter Forty-Seven (or possibly earlier)

Sometimes hope is so frail, so beautiful, like the pattern of a snowflake; and just as easily destroyed. Destroyed is a big word: snowflakes die through melting, through smushing, through sheer inertia. Do nothing and a snowflake dies. How much more does hope strive to live? Perhaps it should die. Perhaps that is the beauty of hope: it only survives in the duration of the moment. Hope might spring eternal, but it falls second by second. Like a series of snowflakes, falling, ever falling, and sometimes rising to fall, swirling to fall, but always destined to fall and to falter, to stop. Become nothing.

There is no splat with snowflakes. But that characteristic is not shared with hope. Hope can be splatted so hard it shakes the ground. Whoever heard of a snowflake causing a ripple? But hope wrenched from the living can tear great swathes of flesh, of pain, and deliver endless rounds of everliving, everdying ripples.

The one and only fumble was in the borrowed merc. His crowning glory was lit up from behind, the streetlight at the end of her road, tucked into a cul de sac, just tall ends of garden walls and not windows overlooking.

She wanted the kisses. She craved his touch, but her images were clothed in softness, and bathed in the same light, that lit up his hair. She did not expect the rasping, the tugging as his desire mounted and hers waned. Those gentle fingers now pulled and probed with a ferocity that frightened her.

Her belt was undone, her blouse pulled up, pubescent breasts lifted from the shelter of her bra. He descended on her nipples and sucked them with an energy that took her breath, but not pleasantly. She tried, God love her, she tried to give an adult response, but it was beyond her. His desire was beyond her. He was beyond her. He was going all the way and so was she, whether she wanted to be a passenger or not. And she did not.

What is rape? She did not say no. Her mind froze. Her body too. When he entered her, the pain seared through her with a vengeance. Hard, dry flesh, entering soft dry flesh; he plunged and she whimpered in pain. He took this for pleasure, or maybe he didn't, but he carried on regardless. He was not raping her, but she was raped. Is there a judgement somewhere for this? She had wanted him, wanted his glorious hair, wanted a kind lover to lie down with. Instead, podgy fingers pulled at her, and he dragged her into womanhood and pregnancy.

I was watching this, although I do not know it now, from the wings. We had all stepped back a bit, we were uncertain if such a union would, should, produce one of us. We slipped guilty glances at one another. The earlier jibes and drunken jollity seemed misplaced. We all wanted to land, like the snowflake, and fall, fall into being, but this dry thrusting seemed, well awful to be honest. I watched her face over his shoulder, and I could have cried. Her big eyes wide with pain, and more than that, with disappointment, with disillusionment. As I stared into her eyes, they opened even wider, and I could feel myself slipping, falling, falling into being. I knew it and then as I became, I knew nothing. I was. Period.

The others, rather than cheering as might sometimes happen, or joking or playing the fool, dissipated quickly. They were relieved not to be chosen this time. Fools rush in etcetera.

Fuck me, I was made and unmade in that moment. A second earlier and I could have been conceived to a princess, a tramp, a weary housewife. Instead, I became daughter to my mother. Is this fate or just plain bad luck?

Chapter Forty-Eight

"Nothing?"

"Nothing"

"Nothing?"

"I said fucking nothing, didn't I."

I am getting angry with Brigid. She is only asking the question. But her repetition is driving me nutty or is it the fact that I still have nothing. Actually, I am not sure what is frustrating me more.

"The conversation with Mother was fucking useless," I say. "After I mentioned his name," and here I shiver as I cannot use the term father or dad or da or anything vaguely paternal, "she clammed up. Just froze and went back inside the house. Refused to talk to me. Said I had tampered with her things. Then nothing. Just turned and walked."

Brigid is thoughtful. I can see her mind whirling. I want to stop it now. Stop her crazy logic.

"I am not talking to Brent about this, no way. I'm serious this time."

"You sure?"

I nod my head emphatically. "The only way I'd get any information out of Brent is to fuck him." Brigid looks shocked. "I'm telling you," I say. "The only way for me to get anything from Brent is to fuck him."

Which is why I'm fucking walking over to the pub now - to face the one person I least want to see, in the foulest mood ever to descend on Ballybawn. I have left George behind, but he is quite happy with Brigid. If it weren't for Mick, I might spread some inter-genus rumours. I still might.

Fuck off reader! What do you think I am? Hey, hold that thought. I know what I am and it doesn't involved fucking Brent for information about my father. So, still fuck off.

"Let's go to Dublin," says Brigid.

"Yes, let's," I agree. "But let's go tomorrow."

"A proper tomorrow? Not a procrastination?"

"Yes, tomorrow."

Tonight, we are in Murphys. Brigid is not that pushed, but then she is not wearing black, and so no neon dandruff problems for her. I am wearing what I thought was safe black; a little black basque which pinches my waist, but I like the way it pushes up my tits. I feel a mix of thrusting womanhood and restoration bosom. Am I saucy wench or vanguard of womanhood? I don't really care and I feel good. I almost strut and I certainly purr. Noel, God love him, has been talking to my tits all night, and I am enjoying great service. We all are.

We arrived about nine thirty. I am feeling slightly pissed now, but very in control, and slightly miffed, but very in control. Pissed, because of the pints I have consumed since we arrived. In control, because my pissed state is harmonious; it is the laughter and humour stage and is well away from inebriety. Miffed, and here I am being fucking honest, because it is only Brigid and Mick and myself; I half expected Liam to be here. There, I said it. And in control because? Fuck me, I am not in control just playing at being in control, which is how my warped brain works. Or did I think that of my former lives? Probably and I am probably just as much in control now, which is not, very not.

Before my self-doubt starts to racket up a notch and before I begin to down the pints at a faster stage, it does happen. The door opens and my eyes are drawn, as they have been all night, to the expectant entrant. At least ten times, the pause, has led to disappointment, although I would not have found the word or confessed to that feeling. Just a hollowness and exhalation of breath and continuation of conversation, not skipping a beat, just carrying on. This time, the familiar shape of his head is there, close cut dark hair, those cheekbones. I turn quickly back to the conversation, not missing a beat, except for my rising, my rising what? Expectation? Excitement? Anticipation? Desire?

Brigid clocks him ten seconds after he arrives. She looks at me questioningly? I look back, eyebrows raised. Is that what was meant to rise? Only my eyebrows?

Her look was priceless, but true. I try not to think about it as I stroke Liam's chest. His cock has risen and fallen, soft now, spent now. I am not having Brigid's conversation now, not while I am with Liam. Right now, it feels right. But I know it is a mess. How much of a mess, I am unsure.

Chapter Forty-Nine

The seduction was easy and all mine. Ignoring Brigid's warning looks, I slipped to the loo and texted him.

"Babe", our code word.

Quickly he responded "Where?" I thought for a moment and decided that I didn't want to meet at the bridge, but then I wasn't sure where else. The post office had been so easy. Oh fuck, "Baileys Bridge" I texted back and rejoined Brigid and Mick.

"You've bloody well arranged to meet him, haven't you?" Brigid was livid. I didn't deny it. I knew full well it was wrong, I was wrong, but it felt so right. How can something that is so wrong feel so right? Obviously, I was exhibiting the classic symptoms enjoyed by all wrong doers. But why was it so wrong? I was tired of playing games, I just wanted. I wanted Liam.

But now, I am here, and he is asleep. His head thrown back and beer-soaked snores whistling through his nose. Right now, I can pretend it is okay. Liam is not awake and not speaking. I don't have to ask for his lies about Fiona. I don't have to evade questions about Jeff. It is, I have to admit to myself, just a bit tawdry. There is a faint whiff of bad behaviour: which is moist and warm and sickly sweet. It's an odour that lies low on the floor, creeping sluggishly between the furniture, occasionally climbing up a chair leg to spray its smell where all good righteous Christian noses live.

I can justify myself but it's an effort and frankly, I'm not sure it's worth the effort. I can do it, just not think about it, nor talk about it.

"I'm not talking about it," I tell Brigid after.

"You bloody well are," she storms. "We bloody well are. Here and now."

I look at her. She is hot and dishevelled. She is so cross. I see the crossness in her, but I am not prepared to talk about it. I think about a) walking off, b) telling her to fuck off and then walking off and c) talking about it. I decide on none of the above.

"Brigid, my friend," I say. "I know what you think. I can see what you think as clearly as if you have written it in four-foot letters above your head. I don't necessarily disagree. But, please, I don't want to talk about it."

I then turn heel, call the dog, and walk out. Fuck I am only twenty-three and for as long as I can remember my life is one fucking mess. I'm due a break soon. Then I remember, with an emotion very close to shame, except I don't do shame, Jeff. I'm not sure what he is – to me that is – but he is the break that everyone deserves. It's time to leave the village for sure. Go and make my way in a grownup world.

I reach the end of the road before it forks. I look around. For a long time. For so long that George actually stops and comes and sits panting at my feet. I look down at him.

"I'm gonna miss you," I say out loud. He wags his tail excitedly. Oh great, even the dog is happy that I am going! I groan, but it's not that funny.

Nor was it funny when Liam woke up. It was nearly three in the morning, and he had slept for forty minutes or so. His first concern was to have a piss. His second was to go home. His third was not to have a conversation. He pulled up his zip, lit a cigarette, and segued out of the picture. It was like a theatrical farce, except I was both audience and dullard, the joke, the butt of his humour which was black. Is that a joke? I didn't mean it to be. If only I had a better sense of humour. If only I'd better taste. It's easy to disguise lust and pretend it's two adults consenting to sex. But really, the consenting bit is overrated. I had been screaming, screaming, but condemned to repeat my conception. I was there but not in the way I wanted to be. Like my mother before me, but I didn't fucking know it, I was repeating a pattern of abuse. Or is abuse a pattern that is handed down, even from beyond the womb? Did the hair colour matter? From golden halo to dark close crop?

As Liam left in a cloud of dust: except it is Ireland and we don't get dust, except for the annual heat wave at the end of May, when everyone's stuck doing exams. And sure, it might be hot for Ireland, but even then, there's not much dust— what with all the rain before, and, naturally, all the rain after.

As Liam left in a cloud of dust: if I could have seen it, that is, since it was, three o'clock in the morning. Or rather, since he had pissed and lit a cigarette, and smoked some of it, it was about twenty past three, and I was trying to talk. God,

Brigid would have been cross, that I was prepared to try and talk to this lowlife and would not talk to her. But it was dark, so she might not have noticed, had she been there, which she wasn't, naturally.

As Liam left in a cloud of fucking dust, which I could not see, and did not exist, I suddenly saw the dust, or lack thereof, was about as insubstantial as we had been.

Dust may swirl up into a vortex: it may choke you, consume you, obscure the truth, clothe you, cover your skin in a fine grey coat; but it is not form. It relies on the wind and the heat to create substance that is as transient as emotion. Cooling, it falls, lifeless, under your feet. Even worse, this is Ireland, so cooling it falls, lifeless, under your feet only to suffer rain and join with mud to become mud. Ashes to ashes, dust to dust, but in Ireland, dust to mud. Same little death. Same petit mort.

I am rubbed thin. Thin as a wafer, rub once more and I tear. If there was dust, I'm sure someone would rub it into me. Into my wound. There is a queue of people with salt, however, jolly helpful people lining up with salt. Great big clumpfuls, slightly dampened in their mouldy paws, ready to push it into me. Push into me and hoping to see the pain. Hate to fucking disappoint them, but I am so thin it travels through, tearing so quickly that the pain is fleeting, a nothing: the damage is done, but the pain is just the tearing, then nothing, gaping holes in my being, flapping in the wind or just falling dripping in the rain. Flittered away until I stand in my bare essence, only the warmth of my breath dividing me from the air beside me, and even that is pulled in and exhaled out, mixing and diluting my formlessness.

PART TWO

Chapter One

Sweet Jesus, I am pregnant. Not literally you understand. Metaphorically. I am crammed full of ideas. I am excited. I am blooming. Actually, all the sushi I have eaten at lunch has swollen my belly, the rice; those innocuous little pearls of rice, sink down into your belly and expand rapidly. I hug my belly, then stoke it. I am lying on the sofa, laptop on my lap, ah, so that's what it's called a laptop for God's sake. It's also the first time I've ever balanced my laptop on my lap. Typically, it gets set up on a table or desk. Now, it has come into its own. How thrilling! How fucking sad am I?

But I'm so excited that even the sadness that is me is happy. I feel like a delinquent. An idiot. I am smiling so hard and typing so fast. I am my own muse. I am writing absolute crap. Go girl, write some more crap. Shit, fuck, shite, crap, turd, faeces, excrement, oh I'm on a roll here. Just tell me to shut the fuck up.

"Shut the fuck up". Shut the fuck up yourself, I'm not stopping until I have written a whole mountain of crap.

Actually, some of it works. Even Karleen says so. Well, she lines up the next three months. I am ahead of schedule. Three months ahead of schedule. I am given more commissions. I am invited to my first celebrity party. I ask Jeff but his answer is just a long look with a raised eyebrow. How come I live with people whose eyebrows can do gymnastics? Must be an attraction thing.

The party is very fucking cool. I like it. I look fucking hot. But I don't pull even the smallest interest, so I have to talk to women all night. That is very strange. I decide the men must be gay. How else do they all look so good, but in a very polished way?

In the bathroom, I stumble across three girls doing a line on the counter. I look longingly, but I am not invited to join them, and I haven't the neck to ask them directly. I ponce in front of the mirror for a bit then leave. Fuck I am cross now. But when I return, Karleen has a ferret-faced man with her. They laugh uproariously when I approach. I open my mouth to complain, to talk, whatever, and she pops an e inside and then leans forward and kisses me on the lips.

"I'm not gay," she says as she pulls away a moment later. I swallow.

"I'm not either," I say fucking firmly, closing my mouth a little too firmly to be funny. She laughs again and as I watch she kisses ferret man also, but on the forehead. He is very small and only reaches her shoulder-ish.

"Hey," he complains.

"I want a Frenchie too."

On impulse I lean over and kiss his angry mouth and slip my tongue in, just a slip, and watch his face as I withdraw. His thin eyes widen ever so slightly. He transfers his attention from Karleen to me, stepping closer. Then looks back at Karleen as if judging the chances he has at pulling both of us. It is very funny. I wink at Karleen, and we gather arms and sway into another room. Ferret man is following, unsuccessfully, at the rear. He is trying to poke his way into the middle of us, but we lock him out. Arriving at another group of polished men, we engage in animated conversation with them, with each other, with anyone but ferret man. It is hilariously funny. I am laughing very hard now. The room is warm and welcoming. I love Karleen, I even think I could love ferret man, but by the time I turn back, he has pissed off, muttering what a nasty pair of lessers we are.

Jeff is awake when I return. I check my watch; it is three fifteen. Not very late, but late enough for him to be still up.

"You're turning into quite the party girl," he says, one fucking eyebrow raised ever so slightly, Cary-Grant style.

I don't know whether to be pissed off, flattered or just annoyed. I don't want to fight. I don't. I am not sure what I want. Really. I wander over to the drinks cabinet. Wander rather than walk, as I seem to have drunk rather a lot and it is only now hitting home. The e must have worn off also as I am very indecisive. Wandering and not sure how I feel, this is not me. I open the door and look inside. I do fancy a nice vodka but I can't be bothered to get ice and lemon and so I opt for brandy instead. So much handier; an all-in-one beverage with a nice taste and great kick. Jeff has large balloon glasses, and I fill a generous measure. I reckon Jeff does not want a drink at this time but still, politely I turn and offer the bottle to him. Shit, he is fucking gone to bed. His empty chair looks balefully at me.

Fuck you Jeff Miller, fuck you.

Chapter Two

Jeff does not carry anger. He sheds it. Quickly and without remorse, but it can be very painful. He is up and gone before I wake in the morning. It is not vengeful. It is not a tactic. It just is. He is. He is gone and I can bloody well put up or shut up. Shape up or ship out.

So of course, I ship out for the afternoon. I am ahead of schedule after all. I meet Tony for coffee. He left the restaurant about the same time I moved to Dublin. There was no correlation, no collusion, just coincidence. I purchase a range of goodies from Tony. I suspect I am one of his better customers. He wants to share some lines now but to be honest, I'm not in the mood. I'm still a bit shaky from last night. Not too bad, but not bad enough for more, quite yet. And not well enough to begin again. As we talk, Tony suggests another coffee. This is to my liking and so I agree but as he gets up, he pats my thigh in passing. Except he was not passing my thigh in the first place. Except as a direct route to my pussy. Oh, fuck. Another complication. I don't want Tony to start making passes at me. I just want to buy stuff off him. I wait until he returns and stare at him aggressively.

"Fuck off," he says. I laugh because I was going to say that to him. "I can read your mind, babe," laughs Tony. "I just copped a feel cause your leg looked nice. Just a friendly feel you understand. You can't blame me, you're gorgeous."

I don't fall for compliments. Fuck off: I am a sucker for compliments. But I don't fall for them. I relish them. I drink them up. I fucking enjoy them. I like them especially when I don't have to give anything in return. That's cool.

And so, two hours later, I am being fucked by Tony in his Dublin flat. I am on the table, legs akimbo, while he thrusts into me, one of his legs also propped on one the kitchen chairs. It is very good, and I am tearing at him, biting his mouth, gouging his back. I cup his buttocks in my hands and pull him deeper into me. He is in so deep; it hurts. I moan a little and squeeze harder. Our skins are wetly slick; even in the frantic thrusting the skins stick a little before pulling apart. Panting, I lean back on my elbows and watch through slitted eyes; I watch his cock slide in and out of me. It is such a thing of beauty.

"Ah Bella, Bella," Tony pants. He leans across the table and drinks his beer, throwing up his head before turning back to me; he kisses me and shares beer into my mouth. No beer spills and I swallow thirstily. "That's my kind of girl," laughs Tony. I reach out to hit him, but he grabs my wrists, both of them, and fans my arms out and up. He thrusts slowly now but very sure, very sure of the pleasure he is giving me and taking from me. I stiffen into the groove. I fucking come into the groove. I relax into the groove. Tony comes into my groove.

"Do I get a discount now?"

"Fuck off"

Chapter Three

I am not sure how much to share with Brigid. She is up for the weekend, and Jeff is away on a course; for 'course' read his annual visit to Jerome. If it seems a little complicated, then it is. Jeff is still a little frosty. We haven't had sex since the night of the party. Or rather, he hasn't had sex since the night of the party. Or rather, I think he hasn't had sex since the night of the party and if he has, it certainly hasn't been with me. I on the other hand am revelling in full on sex with Tony. The bastard still won't do a discount, but the sex is awesome. He is a pussy freak and has turned me in a straight lesser. All I think about is my pussy and what he is going to do to me. I look at Brigid and realise this is something I am probably not going to be able to share with her. Her eyebrows rise anyway.

We are on our way to dinner with Karleen and some of the girls from the office. I am a little worried about compatibility issues. Brigid is the original hippy chick; all falling hair and flowing skirts and bangles. Karleen is much more cocktails in the city chic. But both are good people. So I reckon it'll either be a great success or a fucking disaster but either way it might be fun to watch the fall out. I am tempted to call them 'peeps' but I think that might be a touch Alan Partridgesque; ridiculous to the extreme, but still the appellation rockets through my brain all night.

We meet city centre in Dollys. It is only mildly full but there is a buzz. Karleen, Sue, and Joy are already there.

Within ten minutes, and one large cocktail later, I need not have worried. Brigid is doing her thing, that fucking sailing ship, no her fucking galleon thing, with aplomb and carrying all before her or else washing them in her wake. She is, surprisingly, also a thing of beauty. Surprisingly, as I did not think I would have the same opinion of my friend Brigid and Tony's cock. Was this only the first cocktail? I suppose the e I took before I left, and the two lines of coke might have sprinted me onto this particular comparison.

The night goes well until Brigid turns to me and says, "We are going heffalump hunting tomorrow."

Sudden intuition follows. "I have no desire to find my father, or rather the shit that got my mother fucked up, none."

"Is that the first time I've heard sympathy for your mother?" laughs Brigid. "That's a first."

I turn away angry. Only to get angrier. There is Tony, also in Mollys, but with two women who are not his customers, or rather not just his customers. They are taking turns to rub his leg and laugh into him. It is obvious they are both fucking him, whether together or not is not so clear.

He catches my eye and smiles over but turns immediately back to his company for the night. I turn back to Brigid who is also watching me. What the fuck is going on. Who the fuck is watching whom? The boys watch the girls, watch the boys. Watch the fools, watch the fools. That bloody eyebrow is about to go up, and I decide it is too hard to go there.

"There's Tony," I gush. "Must have moved to Dublin after all." I turn back to our gang and rush in to laugh with their jokes. I am not talking to Brigid again tonight. Nor Tony. I am out with the girls, period.

Chapter Four

"It's called the Panama Disease," I explain to Tony. "It is killing off bananas as we know them." Tony is between my legs and maybe this is not the right time to talk about my next column. He looks up at me.

"What the fuck are you talking about, you crazy bitch. Just lie back and think of Ireland." He shakes his head sadly and resumes tonguing me with epicurean enthusiasm.

Later, I explain again that the Panama Disease is killing off bananas as we know them. The yellow, creamy fruit will soon be gone. Finito. Acres and acres of South America is given over to these fruit, but over specialisation, deforestation, one disease and poof, an entire fruit is exterminated.

"That's where you get the term banana republic," I persist, although Tony is so clearly bored with this line of conversation that he doesn't even try to stifle a yawn.

"Yeah, and it's a clothes shop too," he says. "Maybe they'll rename it, the orange republic or what about the plum republic or apricot? The choice is endless."

I thump Tony. Quite hard. Except when we are having sex, he annoys me quite intensely. And no, it's not a love hate thing. It's just two people who enjoy a good sex relationship and nothing else.

And I'm not upset over the loss of the banana per se. It's just the whole fucking corrupt corporations; the exploitation of the little people. When I tell this to Brigid, she raises her eyebrows so high that they practically slip off the top of her head, like redundant sunglasses. She laughs so hard and for so long that I am moved from irritation to mild amusement and from there to belly laughter. She has stopped laughing and is just sniffing, but I am guffawing like a stuck pig. Eventually, I sober up and continue.

"They had a name," I insist. "Gros Michael. This strain, this monoculture was pretty much fucked in the '60s and they replaced it with the Cavendish. But the disease came back and now the Cavendish is pretty much fucked too."

Brigid is laughing again. "Bring in Dr Who," she snorts. "He'll solve everything."

I'm off again.

Do stuck pigs guffaw? Of course not, they squeal. How the fuck am I going to become a serious writer if I can't even get my cliches correct? I'm as fucked as the bananas. Brigid is not compassionate at all.

"Where did you get that notion that you were going to be a serious writer," she asks, and she is not joking.

"Why shouldn't I become a serious writer?" I counter. There, let her come back with a good answer to that.

"Because it would require serious thought," she says. "And you think with your fanny. Sad but true."

At which point I slap her. No, that's a lie. I think it. It is a fierce and powerful thought that speeds from me. Speeds from me and catches her sharply on the side of her face, knocking her fucking eyebrows off her head.

Brigid guffaws like a stuck pig. "Oh, I got you so good," she squeals. She is mixing her cliches so madly, so badly that I am swimming in bad grammar and polluting the air between us with jagged sentences, misplaced apostrophes and generally bad English. Oh, I so want to be a good writer. "Let's go heffalump hunting," she says. Oh, fuck the grammar, I agree, yes let's go on safari.

Chapter Five

Dear Daddy. I do so hope that we can meet soon. I feel we
may have a connection. You live on a very posh address in
Dublin four and I think, therefore, that you maybe are a
professional of some kind. Of course I am just surmising.
And what does professional mean anyway. The oldest
profession in the world is not exactly what I had in mind. I
think you may be a dentist – although all those teeth are a bit
off putting. Maybe an accountant in some bank or financial
institution? I don't think that you are a doctor. That's the
caring profession isn't it? Perhaps. Your loving daughter,
Bella

Actually, that is such fucking crap. I never thought
those thoughts even when mother was a fucking drunk
alcoholic and lying pissed on her bed and I wanted an escape
route. And especially not now when she is a sober, born again
Catholic with cancer in her hair. Fuck no.

I can safely say that I have no thoughts about the
sperm donor that created me.

Except now, I might meet him face to face. Oh, fuck.

Brigid has brought me to the doorway. Literally. I am
standing here, and I have no fucking clue how I got here. Did
we travel by taxi, or bus? Right now, I could not tell you. I am
shivering. All the lost years come pouring to me and I feel
sick, sick, sick. I'm about to puke. I turn to Brigid to tell her
this, but she mistakes my pallor for the precursor to flight and

rings the bell. I stand impaled by the noise. No ordinary suburban bell, this noise chimes throughout the house, pealing up and down the stairs. It echoes, reverberates, and rounds back to the front door as it opens.

I blink. I blink again. I blink once more. Then I puke my guts up. Over the front step. Over her shoes. It splashes messily into the hall, tiled fortunately, I notice as I open my stomach again. I am blinking each time I retch. The matter from my stomach is almost emptied, and it is then I hear the screams and the shouts. The owner of the black patent pumps, yes I noticed that too, when I was puking, is shrieking.

After, we are not invited in for coffee. Or even water. I have well and truly transgressed the line that Sheila has drawn around her world. The line that separates her and the rest of the flotsam that floats in her vicinity. Sheila is lucky. Her cleaner is working that day. Her shrieks bring her to the door and as we stand in the front garden, I see her mopping and disinfecting the step and hall. Sheila has removed her sick stained shoes. They are put to one side, and I think they will be binned. I am tempted to ask her if this is the case, and if so, can I have them.

Sheila has also just informed us that her husband is dead. If we believe, for whatever ludicrous reason, that her husband was my father, then we should pursue our enquiries through the correct procedures. That we decided to come to her house without any formal procedures is tantamount to stalking and that should we come back again without formal procedures, she would report us to the guards.

Actually, Sheila is a bitch. I can feel the bile rising and help it along. I am puking again, this time with a smile on my face. It hits her skirt this time. As I blink, I see the absolute rage on her face. I decide that I feel sorry for the man who donated his sperm to make me.

We walk away from the elegant, though now sick besmirched, house and gardens. I have recovered but Brigid is very quiet.

"Winnie the Pooh did not find his heffalump either," I point out, in what I hope is a reasonable tone, to Brigid.

I think Brigid is in shock. The only thing which suggests otherwise is that her eyebrows are down. I've never seen Brigid with her eyebrows down, not moving. She is taking slow breaths and talking even slower.

"I think we may have to call it a day," she says to herself.

Chapter Six

Jeff returns. There is a change. I am not a fucking mind reader. He arrives in a taxi from the airport, walks in, throwing his suitcase into the hall. Pours himself a drink: it is only 11 am in the morning. I am hungover and still in my dressing gown. The phone rings. It is Karleen. She is on the phone quite a bit. My earlier pile of excrement has dried up, and she needs more. Actually, I wrote a scatological themed column which she threw out. Spewed down the phone at me. Called me a jumped-up little shit. I guess I should not have contemplated the excrement coming from my editor's ass. It was meant to be jolly. An expose of my editor's merde. It was all those lovely pompous, conceited, jack-assed things: and it poked fun at her, as editor. I was inspired by a famously funny, and very outrageous line at the time, from the early sitcom The Likely Lads. Jack, I think his name was, the bad-ass character, remarked to best mate Rodney that his pretentiously-posh girlfriend was so full of herself that she thought her bottom a perfume factory. The afternoons spent watching sorry repeats had obviously sunk in at some level.

Surprisingly, Karleen, while slating me for my 'kick-ass' column is still looking for another 1000 words. She either likes my shit, you understand, or is looking for value for her advance and her belief in me. I am about to ask Jeff what he thinks, when he tells me there is a change.

"Move out, please" he says. His eyebrows don't rise so he must be serious. Shit Shit. Write about shit and it comes back to you, no need for a fan to slap it about. Oh fuck, fuck. What am I going to do?

"What am I going to do?" I ask Jeff but he is a closed shop. Lights out, shutters down.

I suddenly feel sick. Before I know it, I am puking my guts out in the loo. Jeff stands in the doorway. Concerned but not concerned. He'd like to know that I am going to stop puking but his heart is not in it. He is detached in the same way an ex-boyfriend is. Already. But then perhaps I made him that ex-boyfriend. Or at least pushed him in that direction.

I wipe the salvia threads from my chin. My throat is sore, and I am not sure I have finished puking. There is still some bile in my belly, whether physical or emotional I am not sure. I look at him from the corner of my eye.

"I thought at one stage you were my chance, my break," I say.

"I think that's a little disingenuous, even for you Bella," Jeff replies.

He's right but it doesn't stop me puking again. A dry angry retching from which there is no relief.

Chapter Seven

"You were boning Tony?" Brigid is disgusted. There is a pause, a really, really fucking cross pause, before she asks how Jeff found out.

"I think Tony let it slip." I'm not really sure to be honest. I didn't care per se. I did it. Mea culpa. There's no point crying over spilt milk, or was that spilt sperm, or spilt sick. I wasn't doing too good at keeping body fluids, mine or anyone else's, concealed these days. If I were a crime novel, the readers would have guessed the murderer by the end of chapter one.

I look over at Brigid. She looks so mad she may well be the next murderer. I don't think they'll need Kay Scarletta to solve the murder. I'll have a fucking axe between my eyes with a note attached. 'by Brigid' it'll say. Or 'Bye Brigid' and maybe a little 'x' to show affection, once, before I used it all up in my stupidity.

"You are a fucking disgrace Bella," she says. "I keep on making excuses for you, but this is rotten, stupid, and plain sluttish. How many men do you need at the same time?"

"He's hardly guiltless," I point out reasonably enough.

Brigid looks as though she might argue and then quietens. "I'm so mad," she says slowly. "I'm not saying that Jeff was a keeper, but I thought you liked your new life in Dublin. The parties, the writing, the minor celebrity stuff."

"Very minor," I say. "I got into the odd nightclub free of charge with Karleen, but it also could have been my tits, we'll never know for sure."

Brigid laughs. She pokes my left boob. "Ouch, fuck off, that hurts," I reply retracting like a tentacled sea creature.

Brigid stops midair. Her finger that poked my left boob moves back but points at me instead. She inhales slowly, very slowly. "Oh my God, you're pregnant."

I freeze.

Whose?

Chapter Eight

I pretty fucked up right now. Up the duff, fucked up the duff, just fucked really. I'm also so spaced out it's unreal. Brigid and I had an all-night session. Did we fuck! She put me to bed, and her, but I crept out to the fridge and raided a godawful bottle of organic wine and drank it in silence in the kitchen, on the floor, with only the fridge light for comfort. It was cold admittedly, but it was better than turning the main light on and being caught 'drinking while pregnant'. And I hate fucking warm, white wine, especially godawful organic, warm, white wine.

I touch my belly but it's flat as a pancake. No sign of sprogs there. The only telltale signs are my fucking puking and my tender boobs, oh and no period. But I've never had a regular period so that means fuck all.

All I have in my belly, my womb I should really fucking say, is a fertilised egg. That's all it is. Pregnant. Oh, those fucking big, bellied women falling like dominos, I'm so not there. Period. Fucking full stop. There is a stupid, fat sperm that entered one of my eggs. He didn't fucking knock, and I forgot to put the alarm on. Horacio, please come and investigate this breaking and entry. I don't fucking know. Fuck you Mother.

Chapter Nine

I'm swimming. The water is very blue, very warm. I'm underwater. I don't think I need to breathe. It's very lovely. Oh, fuck, I'm in that film. Finding Nemo. But it's okay really. We're in that current. The one with the turtles. We're swimming, bobbing, splashing along. It's fast but I'm not scared. Neither is…Who is my partner? It's not Nemo. It's not Dory. It's not that tortured fish in the tank. When did I watch the film anyway? How come I know all these characters? Okay, you guessed it, fuck even I guessed it, I'm dreaming. But I know I'm dreaming. How weird is that? I bobbing, surfing, floating on this cartoon current and yet I know I'm dreaming. I'm afraid I'll wake up or just pierce this thin wrapping of fiction in my sleep.

I look cautiously to my left, to my swimming partner. I'm not sure what I'll see. One part of my sleeping brain says it'll be a big fat sperm. And if it fucking is, then there will be a big fat fight. But even my frenzied, screwed-up brain doesn't produce a sperm, thank the fuck! I'd hate to see speared sperm. Would it cry, squeal, or just groan once harpooned? Don't know, don't want to know. Too much information. TMI.

Even though I can't see my swimming partner, I'm still obsessing about that fucking sperm. How the fuck did it creep up on my fucking egg. I thought all my eggs were protected. With guards. Totally impregnable. Fuck that! I've survived 23 years so how the fuck did I get caught. Was it an SAS sperm? And who the fuck launched it?

I'm still on that current. I must be awake, but I'm definitely still asleep. It's not drugs, so this is totally fucked. I'm aware of my legs now. I'm kicking them. In the water. They are very pleasantly tired. I look left again. Why not right? Because my swimming partner is on my left. You fucking moron, why would you want to look right? At the fucking turtles? God help me, who exactly is having this dream?

I look left. It's my Dad. He smiles at me. He's dressed in a long dark coat that floats queerly in the current. But it's not important. He has a moustache. I never knew he had a moustache. Why did no one tell me? Who would tell me? Don't fucking answer that one.

His coat floats strangely. I lean over, as we move along in the current together, and look in. It's like an Aladdin's cave; there are rowing boats, golf clubs, footballs, bits of broken balsa planes, computer games, dvds, football boots, all the debris of life lived with a family. I'm getting a bit bored; it's not my family of course when I spot Winnie the Pooh. Aha!

Aha, fuck what? I nearly wake, spluttering. But some ancient impulse keeps me in the current. Just about. I almost tear open the film, the sticky membrane that holds me in. Aliens here we come, all that claustrophobic cobwebby dripping alien sucking stuff. Tear, tear, and escape, fuck no it's alien and so you're eaten, except for Sigourney. My dream mutates. Not to alien, thank the fuck, but just to a muddy puddle of nothingness. Oh dad, where art thou?

Chapter Ten

Waking is painful. I seem to have a hangover. Not sure from where. I mean I drank a bottle of wine. But I don't get hangovers. Unless the fertilised fucking egg is sending messages to my brain, my body already. Of course, it is. I'm a bit hazy on the whole miracle of life vibe but I do believe it, they, it, the egg, is dividing like mad again and again at an astonishing rate so yes of course it's sending signals all over the shop. I'm all over the shop.

Brigid looks at me, fortunately no longer slumped against the fridge door, but the evidence is in the bin, not the recycling bin, I was so clever to hide it there, not.

"What on earth were you doing?" she starts but I guess she feels sorry for me. Fuck, I feel sorry for me. Very sorry for me. All I can feel, imagine, think about, is the vibrating egg in my womb. It's vibrating as it divides, divides, divides. It's like a cancer. Same principle I think. Excessive dividing and multiplying. Fuck I was rotten at maths in school and here I am a leading expert in the practical application of a theoretical concept.

Buzz, buzz goes my belly, like my phone on vibrate. I've seen the images on television. They're / it's vibrating. Then they pull apart like bubbles: all reluctant, shy, and stretchy, then plop as they tear apart before bubbling back again. Already it's a frogspawn mess in my belly, my womb. I feel a bit weird thinking about the word womb. It sounds so fucking grown up and I don't like it. Wombs are what middle aged, saggy breasted, fat bellied women have. I don't have a womb. Oh no, it doesn't stretch that far. I am just vagina. All pink and perky. It stops after the length of the longest penis. Thus far and no further. I am vagina. Not womb. I'm thinking, letter swap again. Womb to bomb in one letter change, I'm a bomb, bomb shell, bomb shelter, bomb crater, cluster bomb, cluster fuck, bomb fuck. Fuck I can't say even bomb anymore, it doesn't sound right. Actually, it's not the saying, it's the writing. Write it ten times and it looks weird. And as for womb. What kind of word is that? I mean wombat sounds great. I love the thought of wombat. Who named that mammal? Probably the same person who also named the duck billed platypus. What great names. And also, the only egg laying mammal. There's that egg again. Only it's not an egg anymore in my womb-bat. It's a fucking exploding mess of frogspawn, exploding rapidly in my womb-bat.

When I think about the multiplication, I wonder. If it's dividing and multiplying so fast, why doesn't it run out of womb space in, say, a thousand sums? Does each division result in smaller and smaller units? I mean, are we talking ever decreasing units or what?

My head is exploding. Fuck my womb-bat! But that, I believe, would be like closing the stable after the horse has bolted.

Chapter Eleven

Today I'm breaking the law. I'm breaking the law. I'm up on the moor. With George. The mad unputdownable George. Who has welcomed me with as much enthusiasm as he left me. God, but that dog is consistent. I'm leaving you George. Yes, yes. I'm home again, George. Yes, yes.

I'm walking the law. I'm waking the law. I'm walking the land. Lawing the land. Landing the law. Landing the blow to the jaw. Arms swinging, I'm breaking the law. I've broken the law. It's there. Shattered in my imagination. Bleeding from between my legs. Shards of frogspawn coated in globules of congealed blood. That'll stop your fucking division.

I'm swinging my arms. Striding my legs. I'm walking the unputdownable George. I'm walking the unstoppable division. It's hard to walk with such activity clouding my womb. Clouding my head. Dividing my thoughts. I'm unputdownable but is my mess of division equally so?

"Divide, divide," says George. "Conquer, then conquer." I'm puzzled until I realise he's talking to my frogspawn. How dare he? How dare he bypass the solid, indivisible mass to talk to the amorphous gloup that is fermenting in my middle?

And I feel a shuddering reply. A movement like a wave as the thousands, is it millions perhaps already, of cells call back to George. But each voice only lasts a second before it too divides and calls and divides again. Echoes call back, but so many, so many. How can I break the law with so many, break so many? I feel their quickening. Their living. The quick and the dead and these are very much alive. They are dividing faster than ever. It is an army of cells ever breaking, every dividing, but I feel something else too. A solidifying. Even as they divide, my frogspawn, it is becoming denser. Thicker. Less, a they and more of an it, a thing. Unified. United. Uniform.

Chapter Twelve

The birds are not singing anymore. There is a silence. I am alone and palely loitering. There is a silence. Unputdownable George is down. Put down by himself. Crashed in a messy sprawl of legs and panting tongue.

I stand in the forest and balance my thoughts. I am so bereft of answers. I don't even know where to start with the fucking questions. I am emotion. I am feeling. I am pale. I am at my core. I am more than my core. I am more than one. Not yet two, but one plus something. I wasn't any good at fucking fractions either.

I am angry. I want to pull into my belly. Into that wantonly named womb and tear the cluster vibrating on the wall, tear it off with my bare hands. Tear it off and throw it to the ground. For God's sake George would pounce on it and devour it one mouthful. Here I am cluster. Yes, yes. Here I am eaten. Yes, yes. God, but that dog's consistent. George looks at me. But he addresses the cluster. Again. Not me. Fractionate. Fractionate. He pleads. God, he's even coining new words.

The hum rises again. The silence is turned into a hum. The birds sing in the trees. There is noise in the forest. And the cluster is fractionating wildly, spinning wildly, turning, turning into me. It is me. Little pieces of me, dividing, dividing, fractionating, humming. The wave rises and rises. It pours over me in vibrating echoes. It is me calling to me. Why did I not see it before? Feel it before. Tell it before.

"I'll sing you a fucking lullaby," I laugh suddenly out loud. "Today is stayed. Tomorrow is another story." George looks at me quizzically.

Tomorrow is another fucking day. I live to fight another day. My fraction lives to fight another day. The hum is consistent still. They, it is still vigilant. There is no real trust yet. I don't trust me so why the fuck should the cluster? The button has been pushed. The egg pierced. The process begun. There is no turning back, except for the lilies of death. The knives of death. The backstreet death. Le belle dame. She is poised with her knife. Or am I poised with my knife. Am I the watcher? I don't know. Am I the surgeon, the hacker, the incisor? Do I stay the arm, mine or hers? Yes, I stay, the cluster stays, but whose arm is stayed?

Today I am conquered. The sedge is withered from the lake but the birds do sing. They sing in reply. They give thanks. They give merci.

Chapter Thirteen

I am puking my guts up. For the third time since 4am. Every hour on the hour. I am so fucking tired of being sick. It feels like my fucking mouth is raw from stomach acid. How did those fucking stick insects with bulimia do it? My throat is sore, my eyes bright red and swollen, my belly rumbling with fatigue and cramping. Not more sick, not again. Even when it is finished, it's not really finished, I still feel the residual sickness washing round my belly. Even though I have finished, I have not finished, I feel a sensation like toxic waste fermenting in my belly. Batter my belly why don't you. For when you have done, you have not done, for I have more.

Brigid is beside me. She is beside herself. I am beside myself. The tears course down my face. It is the stream of sickness. I am not crying but my retching has emptied my eyes, my lacarma are dry and squeezed. I sit back on my heels and breathe, slowly and painfully. She pats my hand. My hand is resting on my thigh. She pats it sadly, shaking her head.

"This too will pass," she half whispers. "This too will pass."

I nod back. "I'm going to the doctors today," I say. I note her rising eyebrows and stay them with a smile. "I'm going to sign up for the pregnancy," I say. And as I say it, I know it is true. I have made up my mind.

Chapter Fourteen

It's tougher being pregnant than it looks. Because right now I don't look pregnant at all. So it looks normal. I look normal. I don't look pregnant. I don't act pregnant, except for the puking and that is largely a solitary function. George sometimes looks in on me. Brigid is often on hand, but also at a remove. She can't help and I don't want her to watch. And there is only so much hand and back patting that a friend can do.

My first quandary is to find out who the father is. This is somewhat a philosophical quandary as I prefer to choose the father, than have the father foisted on me and my unborn child. Brigid says this approach is totally untenable, ridiculous and quite farcical. I agree, but I'm going to do it. There are four serious choices, unless I add in the fifth, that of an immaculate conception. I argue this point also quite strongly in the kitchen. Just because I have slept with men, does not mean that God has not chosen me for his vessel. That's a double negative Brigid points out to George. Was Mary chosen just because she was a virgin, or was it because she was Mary? Brigid gives up on orthodox argument, but Mick is coy.

"Did you see an angel?" he asks. "Did an angel tell you that we were carrying the son of God?"

"An angel may well have visited me and told me that I am carrying the daughter of God," I point out reasonably enough. "But I'm not prepared to say if this is true or not. Not at this stage."

"At what stage might you be prepared to concede ordinary conception?" Mick asks.

I don't genuinely know. I like the idea of not having to deal with an earthly, human father. Wouldn't it be nice to refer matters directly heavenward?

"Wait till your father hears about this?" I will threaten in a rage. Then realise that of course her heavenly father would know she was bold even before she was bold. Even before I knew she was bold.

For when she was bold, he'd know she's bold, for he has more.

Chapter Fifteen

If the father of my unborn child is not God, then it might be one of four mortals. It actually might be one of a few others, but if I'm not prepared to acknowledge fatherhood through physical DNA, then I'm surely not prepared to even countenance the possible parenthood of some randomer. I have dismissed those fly by nights from my mind and suggest you do also. It won't do any good raking up their names or even just their faces. They are no longer part of my jigsaw, my life. They are gone, period.

So, I return to the scene of the crime, if crime it be. I offer you Brent first of all. Why not? He is after all the legally married spouse of Bella. It might be a good match. We are married still and that might make it easier for the unborn child. I think about the last time I had sex with Brent. But it's not really a good memory. I decide that I don't want my unborn child conceived on iffy sex. Then there is the iffy relationship with Marie and her subsequent demise. And to top it all, mother's habitation in his house. No, it's so not you Brett.

Thinking of sex, my thoughts fly to Tony. But do I want a drug dealer to be father to my unborn child? Nor did any of our couplings have anything to do with procreation. Recreation, yes, procreation definitely not. Not really, it's okay now but I can't see any long-term security in it, or in him for that matter.

Jeff? No. He has a child and guilt in spades. Besides, he threw me out, that's not good. A man has to respect the mother of his unborn child and it's not nice to chuck her out in the street. Okay, he didn't know but still, he did the chucking of me even while I was chucking my guts out.

So that leaves Liam. God help me. God help Liam.

Chapter Sixteen

How does one catch a fly? Not with a swat, that's not. How does one catch a butterfly? Not with a jar, for sure. How does one catch a fish? Put salt on its tail, of course. Put salt on its tail and dance a tale and spin and spin.

Nothing has changed in Ballybawn, except for my womb. And since that is firmly hidden inside my flat belly, nothing has changed in Ballybawn. I walk down the main street and look at my old neighbours. Even the young ones are old. They have that tired look. It's a look they begin to wear during their teens, then it solidifies, it stays with them. It doesn't matter if they are laughing or crying. Maybe they have moments when it tears, stretches, or cracks a little. Maybe during childbirth, or at the moment of orgasm, or at death. Maybe it is rendered asunder only with great emotion. But these people of Ballybawn don't look as though they are capable of great emotion. It is put away like the good dress or the brave hat and only taken out for weddings and funerals.

I feel like a spinning top in this drab little street. My colours are turning so fast, they are blurred into a rainbow of show. I am not sure if it is the return or the quivering mass inside me. I am positively glowing. I've gone right past blooming and straight into neon lights blazing. People walking towards me are dazzled with the light. They duck instinctively as they approach, shielding their eyes from my light. Some cross the road to avoid me, while others bravely walk alongside me, up to me and past me, but I can see the strain in their walk, the way their arms move a little more forcefully than is necessary, the way their eyes are hooded and avoid me.

"You're a fathead!" screeches Brigid when I get home. "What do you think you are? The Blackpool Illuminations?"

I sniff. But yes, that is what I think I am. I am radioactive, nuclear active, baby active. I need to seek out Liam. Seek and destroy that trollop of a girlfriend. Pull him into my spinning orb, sprinkle a little salt on his tail, and reel him in.

"Fathead," repeats Brigid, sniffing too but with laughter.

It is George who has to point out my radioactivity is really plain scandal and gossip.

"It is sticking to you like toilet paper," he points out in a very pleasant and kind voice.

His baleful eyes soften the truth, and he dribbles a bit, perhaps at the thought of chasing toilet paper in the park, perhaps imagining himself as the Andrex puppy, all bouncing and cuteness. And he is right. As I walked up that street, whiffs and sniffs floated out of windows, from offices, from people walking past. There were trails wrapped round my legs, making me shuffle as I walked. And the people ducking away from me were not hiding from the light but chucking loo paper bombs from behind twisted lips and through curled and vicious expressions.

I go to bed and put the salt in my wounds. It is not a fish I have caught but a wound. And a load of shitty toilet paper. The salt stings but it cauterizes the wound. And sterilises the wound. And cleans the shite. Well, it provides a barrier to shite. I'm baking my fish in salt. Must have learnt more from Jeff than I gave him or me credit for. Except I don't have my fish. First catch your hare. First catch your fish. First catch your breath.

Chapter Seventeen

"Finding a father for your unborn child is not technically an occupation," Brigid says. I look at her from under the duvet. "Says who?" I'm not budging. I'm staying put.

"Says me," and she expertly flips the duvet off me, from my clenched fingers, and off the bed onto the floor where it lies in a cosy puddle.

I, however, am still on the bed, cold, bollock naked, freezing and pretty fucking hacked off. But I have learnt from experience that shouting does not work with Brigid. Resistance is futile. Resistance is pointless. Mine is not to make reply. Mine is not to reason why. Mine is but to do or die. Into the valley of the bathroom, ride me and whose army.

That gloopy shower is still there. It has not benefited from my absence. Not at all. I am surprised that I do not morph into Frankenstein, or Friedastein, all those crackles, all that gloop, all that lack of bleach. Cleanliness may just be an absence of dirt. Or it may be nearest to Godliness. Either way, it is to be desired. And the absence of which is much missed by me.

I look in the steamed-up mirror. I check for the fucking toilet strands. They appear as fronds in the mirror. Fronds of steam. Clean in the steam. Either the shower has worked, or I am impervious inside Brigid's house. I am not sure which is the case, but it is good to shower, however precariously, and yes. Brigid I am up, and I am showered, and I am ready to face the day.

Which is just as fucking well because I have a visitor. Mick informs me. Mick is a prick. Mick says it is a man. Which is true and does not make Mick a prick by virtue of that information alone. But Mick is not stupid. Or maybe Mick is stupid. But he knows that if he says I have a visitor and it is a man, I am going to think one of four fathers. Okay, you guessed it. There is a flaw to my argument. I am somewhat fixated on my search and all I want to see is fathers. Or rather the Father of my unborn child. So, I go back to Mick being a prick. He says there is a man to see me. Actually, I am the stupid one. See, how I won't call myself a prick? Good work, woman, there are too many people queuing up to call me names, so I shall not help them. So, perhaps I am stupid like a prick, because I want to see the pussy, see the money, show me the money, show me the father. I think in some small recess of my brain, because I have willed Liam to be the father, he will appear, magiced out of my wanting. Or at least one of the rejected fathers will appear, supplicant and needy, only to be rejected, or at least to be put onto my waiting list.

No, instead a small weedy, teenage boy awaits me. He is not father. He is not even father material. His floppy hair is cute but fatherish? No.

Of course, he is not fatherish. He is actually brotherish. Actually, or actually according to him, he is brother.

What the fuck! I have been searching for father – my father, my child's father – and I have unearthed brother. How fucking strange is that?

Chapter Eighteen

He followed the trail like Hansel and Gretel. He saw the treads of toilet paper floating through the forest and he came here. He is shivering and I want to hold him, make him warm. Instead, it is Brigid that does that. She does it. I watch my brother, my brother shivering, but hesitate and yet want to hold him and want not to hold him. He is not child, but he is not man either. From a boy to a man there is a terrible stretch. Worse than the breaking of voices and the dropping of gonads. It is the putting away of childish things and the taking up of manly chores. And it is a very fierce path, worse than for a girl in some ways.

Watching Bob awkwardly remove himself from Brigid's embrace, I look at his face for signs of mine. I see fear, resolve, upset, anguish, anger – a rake of emotions but very little of me, of my face, of my phrenology.

I am ten years older than Bob. Bob is ten years younger than me. He is fourteen and tall and skinny and spotty. He has large hands with bitten nails. His eyes are big to the point of bulbous, no slits there. But his lips are mine. Or rather our father's. They are round and plump and red. Moist in a teenage boy is hardly attractive to me. Moist in a pregnant woman, the same. Our Father's Lips. Hallowed be our name. Thy kingdom come, thy will be done, on earth as it is in heaven. Our father in heaven, or wherever, cursed be thy name. Forever be your shame. Not in the making of me, not in the heavenly love, but the fucking running away afterwards.

Then, his namesake didn't hang around for Mary either, did he? Left that poor sap Joseph to pick up the pieces and carry the load. Only my poor fucking mother had no one to step into her ambit. No angel to appoint a man to put her on a donkey and carry her to love's labour lost. The utter unfairness of it has even me saddened.

Bob is not dwelling on my lips, our late father's lack of responsibility, or even my slit eyes. He has run away and wants to stay. My projectile vomit episode at his mother's house clearly made an impression on him. He did not witness it of course but suffered many renditions told by his mother, each version gathering pints of vomit so that even the Liffey would have been put to shame by my prodigious output of puke.

I don't think we want another person staying in our already cramped and not very tidy house. I don't need an underage minor staying with us. I don't think the police or the child protection services or whatever would look very kindly on us. But from my extreme and advanced maturity, I remember the child that was me. God, does sarcasm kick in once you hit the twenties. When did that happen to me?

"What the fuck," I say. "Let him stay a night or two. Breathing space. Living room."

"Lebensraum," says Mick a bit darkly for me. Actually, a bit fucking smartly for me, because I have to get Brigid to explain afterwards. And Bob is as far away from Hitler, or a Hitler youth, as you can get. I decide, before utter fatigue catapults me into my bed, that I quite like my little brother. He hasn't said more than ten words and that helps too.

Chapter Nineteen

If looking for a father for my unborn child is not an occupation, then perhaps looking after my kid brother counts? I don't want to give him back, I decide. He slept on the sofa and is still there, hair tousled under the duvet and watching the television. Reality television, my favourite kind, not.

"Does your mother know?" I ask him. "I can't take a chance on a kid like you."

He is way too fucking young to know what the fuck I am talking about. Hey, I am way too fucking young to know. Except of course, like bad pennies, stuff rolls around and comes around every generation or so. And even the bad stuff becomes good stuff. Or was it always good stuff? I'm not sure. But I know second time, third time round, it gets credibility that it might not have had the first time round. I guess it's called survival. And since I do survival, I salute you bad pennies. Bad pennies of Ireland, I salute you. Bad pennies of Sweden, I fucking salute you too. I guess it's called revival.

Those pennies, they think I'm taunting them. They're angry. They're upset. Michael Cain is swearing at me. I'm not taunting you Michael. I'm not. I'm admiring your bravery, your stamina, your 'once more unto the breach dear friends'. And there the fuck I am, jumping up and down with my Zulu pals thomping the dry ground with hardened feet, dust rising, voices rising, spears rising but only in salute.

Of course, in Ireland we didn't have Zulus. We had the pope who came to a packed field to ensure that twenty years later we have more John Pauls than any other nation in the world. Young People of Ireland, I love you. Young people of Ireland ensure my name lives on. Conceive now. Conceive quickly. Conceive with my name, even for girls.

Really, I'm surprised I'm Kathleen and not Josephine Pauline. I wouldn't put it past my mother; except she was not inspired by the pope at the time of my conception. Fighting for her reason was not the same as being inspired by the Vatican.

I look at my brother, and he starts to ask to stay. Or rather his puppy dog eyes do the trick. Better slow down boy. That's no way to go. Does your mother know? Take it easy. Take it easy. Try to cool it boy. Play it nice and slow. Does your mother know? And I'm not fucking dancing with you honey!

Chapter Twenty

It is my mother who decides after all. While I struggle with my newfound fecundity which stretches far beyond the womb, she is slowly removing the hooks and tackle that attach her to life. I am growing life inside me and adding family members with the wilful abandonment of a preschool toddler. Draw a picture of your family. Ok, teacher. Here is mother, though her picture is very shady now, but look, I have added my little brother and a father, also a little shadowy I have to say. And there is the wicked stepmum, she is very clear and dressed all in red. Are there others? I'm a little hazy on that point. Bob, my little stepbrother, is an only child, with three sisters whom he does not like, at all. I like his style, except I am in addition mode now, not subtraction. You can't leave them out, Bob, I admonish him. They are staying in my new family portrait.

But, as in all things, in my poor benighted, fucked up life so far, it is my mother who decides. She is officially in treatment now. She has been through the nuclear mill, the radioactive mill, the chemical mill. They have zapped her with lasers intended to kill entire fleets of klingons. They have pumped enough poison into her body that would choke the Shannon. Her hair has fallen out. Her body cannot eat anymore, cannot break down the merest titbits that pass her lips. She puts a spoon to her mouth and a single rivet of thin soup dribbles in. Her tongue is gatekeeper to her mouth, and it pushes the watery liquid around until, reluctantly, it releases the swallowing impulse so it can travel down into her ravaged stomach. And even there, the bile bubbles and rocks and threatens to spew the droplets back up again. It is a torture to eat, but what is the alternative? Right now, mother is not bothered with the alternative. Bring it on, she says. Bring it on.

She is home now, or rather in Brent's home, never really my home. He is doing a bit of a blinder but I am wholly unconvinced as to his motives. It is enough just to punish me? I watch him from the corner of my eye. I am here now. Bob in tow. Brigid has sent us, or rather me, but Bob is not to be separated from me, not for a moment. He is champion, boy soldier, small knight on white horse. When I knocked at the door and Brent opened it, his first reaction was so obvious. I did not disabuse him of his notion of boyfriend. Why should I? I introduced him as Bob, why should I not? Bob, he heard. Bob, does she find you strangely attractive? He thought. It was written in large capitals above his head, in a thought bubble that vibrated with pulsing energy.

Now, we are standing in the sitting room. Bob is attached to me with invisible threads like a spider's web. Whenever I move, he shimmys alongside me in an unchoreographed dance that has little appeal to a watcher. Certainly, none to Brent, for it has all the characteristics of a lovers' private two step and none of the beauty of a ballroom exhibition. It is a clumsy, bumping motion that somehow keeps in step, like two lovers tearing at each other, and rolling across the bed in a synchronicity that only stops short of one falling out or over or on.

Bob, do I find you strangely attractive? I look at my shadow. He is attraction itself. He is colt, that awkward bonding of legs and arms and skinny chest. How do I love thee Bob? As a sister but with the intensity of a lover. I look at him. His bright blue eyes burn with the same intensity back. There is nothing to bond us but blood. But there is also nothing to disappoint us for we had nothing and where nothing dwells, expectations have no chance to sprout and rot in the self-same season. We are wasteland and we thrive in the dry arid soil. Leaning together, lie in on me, I say silently, lie in on me.

Mother is seated beside the fire, covered in a rug against the heat of the room, but she is shivering with the cold. My coat is off, and I am hot. My cheeks are burning against the heat and against the sparrow head that is my mother. She opens her eyes. Then closes them. I am fences up, full alert on, snipers in position, SAS crack unit at the ready. Oh, please not more shit. Please, I beg.

Eyes still closed, she says her name for me. "Kathleen" and she sighs. "The prognosis is not good. The treatment was not enough. It has killed me but not the cancer."

She stops and it is Brent that fills in the rest. The cancer has spread; it's the whole enchilada. It's having a fucking party in my mother's body. She is the best fucking host in the entire village. Cancer has entered every part of her, the party spills into the kitchen, the garden, the upstairs bedroom where some very naughty coupling is taking place. It's a party to end all parties. Fuck, it really is the party to end all parties. They're at the 2am, in the morning state where drunkenness is taking hold. Conversations are slurring and repetitive. There is a man in the kitchen chatting up a very drunk bird.

She is so drunk he has to hold her up against the fridge or she will fall. Her eyes are spinning but she has great tits. He is watching for his moment to take her outside, push her up against the wall and grab a shag. In the cloakroom, there is an underage teenager who is puking his guts up. He's not meant to be there of course, but by now he doesn't fucking care. He just wants the puking to stop. His stomach is raw, and the cloakroom is rank with vomit. He will pass out shortly, slumping against coats with a slick of vomit at his feet. But since this is a party to end all parties, there won't be anyone checking out. The coats will stay there and so will the boy.

In the drawing room, an earnest middle-aged man is talking politics to a disenfranchised woman. His breath smells a little, he has a paunch, and he rubs his ear vigorously each time he makes a new point. She is recently single, newly divorced and eating for comfort. She is glad of his attention but all the while she is saying to herself, is this it? Did I swap my shithole of a marriage for this? Because this is not so much better than her sweaty ex-husband. Not much better at all. She has straightened her hair, got a manicure and dressed up to the 'tens', albeit in a dress size larger than when she left the marriage and the 'nines' to a previous life. Is this it? She wonders again, before taking another drink. Alcohol to dull the disappointment of a life begun again with all the lackluster of a sparkler at an office party. We have tested and tasted too much lover, through a chink too wide, there comes in no wonder.

This is the longest I have stayed in my mother's company in a long while and not been upset, angry or just plain pissed off. It may be because she still has her eyes closed. It may be because Bob is there, and I am trying to set a good example. It may be because I am enjoying Brent's discomfort as he tries to gauge the intensity between Bob and me. I think he's beginning to twig. We are blood and not sex and that is probably pissing him off even more – that he mistook our connection in the first place.

Again, it is Mother who decides. She opens her eyes and looks at me. Then her eyes pan away from me, across the room, and takes in my shadow. For the first time she becomes aware of Bob's presence. Her eyes open wide, frightened and she looks round the room in fear for what? I'm not sure but Brent moves over to her quickly.

"It's okay Pamela," he says. Patting her hand.

God, but I hate that man. Platitudes. Never let him get near enough to pat my hand, please God, I, confirmed heathen, pray to nameless beings, distressed out of my poor little mind to wonder at my sudden shift in belief.

Mother looks again at Bob. "George," she says in a scared voice. "George?" and her voice rises querulously.

I am suddenly thrown from quasi compassion to full blown rage. I am not sure why. "It's Bob, Mother," I say. "We are lovers."

Before Bob has a second to even figure out what I have said, am saying, I drag him, bonds forgotten, dance finished and exit stage left. Brent catches my arm as I leave.

"You…" he starts to say only I look him back right in the eye.

"If it's sauce for the gander, it's sauce for the goose," I spit at him, detach my arm and leave with my lover, Bob. HAHAHAHA. What the fuck have I done. Actually, it is Bob who is cool. He laughs hard as we fall onto the street.

"You're a fucking bitch Bella," he laughs. "Why do you hate her so much? Why are you so fucking mean?" But he is laughing so I start to laugh too.

"Have you a lifetime and I'll tell you," I shout at him. We are running now down the street away, away like the lost boys. We don't care. We run. We shout. We'd fly if we could. "She drove away George, my father," I say at last. We have stopped running and are lying against a wall, panting. "I never met him, except as an egg." I tell Bob. It is my serious voice, but I am echoing my own unborn child's condition. I want to tell Bob about my baby-to-be. I want him to be … uncle. Wow there is a thought.

"But Dad visited you until you moved away from Dublin, when you were about three or so, when Angela was born."

The fucking sheet is torn again. The sheet in the temple. Torn in two. What the fuck? When I was three? I knew my father until I was three? Why until then and no more? Ding dong dell, Pussy's in the well.

Chapter Twenty-One

I am raw. The fraternal umbilical cord was only severed when I was three. I clutch my knees, hug myself, and cry for what I had, and lost, and never fucking knew. He read Winnie the Pooh to me. From some dark recess of my brain, I know that now. But who tore him from me? My mother or Bob's mother? Was he called to be father of his legitimate child? Leave behind the bastard offspring of feckless couplings. Cleave to the newly discovered world of guilt free fatherhood. Bastard. How he ruined the path. Left me to the devices of a drunken teenage mother. I'm swimming in porridge. I can't see which way is up. I don't know if I'm swimming or drowning or just waving.

It's Bob who comforts me. His skinny arms hold me tight. He's fucking scared. He hasn't a fucking clue but some instinct in him tells him not to let go. I barely feel him. I don't see him. I am rolled into a ball. I'm a rolling stone. I'm gathering no moss.

We dance our new dance for hours. All night. It's a lover's dance without the sex. We are cleaving. Cleaving together our blood. Grieving together our pain. Weaving together our lives. Leaving our father behind us. Sometime near dawn his skinny arms release their hold, fall away. His exhausted body lies on the bed, breathing deeply as he sleeps, cheeks flushed, mouth slightly open. I pull away, gently tearing the bonds that bind us. The bonds fall in wispy strips on the bed, stirring slightly in the warm air, then settling softly back on the covers.

I pull on my coat. I walk outside. It is very cold. It is very dark - darkest before the dawn. I walk. Head down. Heading out. I head for Bailey's Bridge. In my fug I wonder. I wonder who will greet me there. I decide to up the odds, fish out my phone and text 'babe'. It is a long, long time since I texted his number but it feels familiar and warm. And I am not surprised when I get a reply. This is inevitable. It is very dark, it is very late, or rather very early, of course, he will reply. I tell him where to come but he is already on his way. This is madness, where was he before, that he is on his way? Is he detouring for another rendezvous? Or anticipating my call? Or is he always ready and waiting for me?

Right now, I'm looking for answers. But the right answers. Not to the stupid incidental questions that plague us like dandruff. No, the big fucking serious stuff.

He is on the bridge before I arrive. I see his cigarette burning in the ebbing darkness. I see his silhouette against the growing light. I have a very important question for him.

I frame it in my head. Will he be the father of my unborn child, of his unborn child? Will he love it and cherish it until his death? Will he bestow his worldly goods on it? Will he love it and never leave it, so help him God?

I reach him. I look into his eyes. I take his hand and place it on my belly. I hold it there and look into his eyes. Comprehension falls like snow, softly whirling round us, gently falling, sticking to our faces. I want to kiss the flakes on his cheeks, touch his temple, frame his face in my hands,

.

frame my question in his mind, frame the answer, and take his oath.

Here we make our vow, I say silently. He nods. I look over towards the edge. Here I will come if you break your vow, I say silently. He follows my gaze but pulls me back again. Here I come to worship your body, he says silently, and my body inside you, inside you and growing. Here I come to worship what we have made together. Come to me and I will destroy you with love, he says. I will break you up so you will never love another. Make you up so you will never need another. I will break you and make you and make you mine forever.

This is my vow, he says.

You have mine already, I say.

Chapter Twenty-Two

"Life is very complicated." I say.

"Only if you make it so," says Brigid.

Bob says nothing. He is not talking to me. I have let him down. I have replaced him in the hours before dawn. In the very darkness before dawn, when all things are at a low, when the dying come to die, when the fortress breaks down, when the tunnel collapses. He fell asleep on duty and feels the victory as painfully as defeat. For him, it is defeat. He curses himself for letting go, for giving way to sleep, for loosing the bonds. He had manned the fortress, kept it safe, found himself to be champion, a gatekeeper, a guardian. Now, it was all for nought. He was destroyed by that which came in the night, like a thief, and stole his role away, stole his prize away.

"He is a child," I say to Brigid quietly. "He was a child before he came here," she says. "He is a child no longer."

"I am with child," I protest. "I cannot mother another."

"It is not mothering you offered him," says Brigid and I feel her anger rising. "How many people must you trample in your way? Can you not see what you do? Can you not see it? There is a path littered with your human debris, all maimed and injured and cut. Can you not see it?"

"There is nothing to see," I say coldly. "It is a flesh wound, nothing more." I look over at Bob to confirm my words but once I look, I am guilt-ridden. There is a gash to the side of his head. I have inflicted it. With an axe or some other violently cutting blade without subtlety. It is very red, very bloody and very raw. I am ridden with guilt. Guilt is on my back and tearing clawfuls of flesh from my shoulders, my back, my head, anywhere it can reach.

This is a new experience for me. Even as I am ridden by the bastard guilt, I try to push it away. I look away. I move away. The creature pulls harder, tears harder. I am frozen in a moment. I am frozen in a frame. I leave my body and turn and look back at the tableaux. There is Bob curled up on the sofa.

Watching TV. He does not look at me but his very not looking is reproach beyond bearing. There is Brigid looking at me with real and righteous anger on her face. She is adoptive mother, and I am spoilt teenager. Her eyebrows are so high, they might audition for the Cadbury's Advertisement. There am I, half turned from them both, the pain from my guilt monkey etched on my face. But it is George that says it all.

"Woof," he cries. "What a load of bollock!" And he jumps round the room excitedly. "I want a guilt monkey too," he says.

But dogs live in the moment, and I don't think they feel guilt. And even if he did, he would outlive the moment so fast, his new best friend would be there and gone in a matter of seconds. But hey, how come George is moving when we are all frozen in the frame? Dogs, huh, they're so clever!

Chapter Twenty-Three

I have things to do. People to see. Places to go. I am all action. I am action. I am action girl. I just can't wait to get going. I toss and turn all night. I am trying to plan and it's just not going according to plan. But I'm going to action it, make it plan, make it work. First Bob. I wake him up from his slumber.

Tossed curls, heavy breathing, still in his tee shirt, asleep on the sofa and I expect he only went to sleep very late. His arm is flung above his head and he is the very picture of pubescent hormones, all quivering slightly in his sleep, forming a glow about his body and a faint odour, a masculine spill of pheromones that crawls across the room in a slow rolling wave.

I shake his arm, and he throws it back across his chest, swatting me away like a bothersome insect. I shake him again, this time on the shoulder. He opens his eyes briefly, sees it is me, and closes them crossly again. His face is set into a scowl.

"Bob," I begin with my prepared speech, but I don't get very far.

"Fuck off," he says through gritted teeth.

"Bob," I try again. He groans and turns over. Something tells me he doesn't want to talk to me. But I want to talk to him, so I persevere. "I need to talk with you."

He opens his eyes, but he is so pissed off. It is written all over his face and his body language. His whole body is screaming at me to fuck off. Fuck right off says his elbows as they jut out at me. Fuck off says his right knee as it angrily crosses his left. His right foot flips forward and back, piss off, it says repeatedly. Just piss off. Get lost. Don't want to talk to you. His chin squares and he looks at me from under darkened eyebrows. They are twitching so much they could give Brigid a run for her money. I take a step backwards under the combined body language and the air is blue with imprecations.

"Bob, I'm having a baby," I start. And then I stop for I am not really too sure what else I want to tell him, need to tell him. "And I went to the father last night, and he has agreed," I say. "He has agreed to stand by me. He is going to be the father of my child and is not going to run out after he finishes the House at Pooh Corner. He's going to be for keeps."

It's quite a speech. I almost expect applause but there is silence. A fairly flat silence that is dead. Dead with emotion, dead bodies, in a sea, dead corpses, bobbing, in a sea. There has been a shipwreck: I am that shipwreck and all around me are corpses, floating in the moving water. I can't believe I've killed so many people. So many emotions, so many dreams and hopes. Of course, Bob is a teenager, and he has more emotions to kill than most, than most dead adults. But I'm doing a good job of killing him faster than most.

"You told me to lie in with you," he said. "I know I came unbidden, but we coupled like needy plants that grow to a single light. We cleaved and clung and wetted the bond between us, cemented the bond between us, fermented the bond between us. I thought we were making fine wine, but you were only making vinegar."

Actually, he said fuck all. He looked at me as if I had three heads and took off. He locked himself in the bathroom, and I wanted to warn him about the fungicidal growths, the gloop, and the shower poised to electrocute the whole fucking neighbourhood, let alone the one poor fucker shivering in its cold and pitiful stream. But Brigid had walked into the room. Her eyebrows, and here I just want to kill Cadburys, said a whole fucking volume.

"Are you out of your cotton picking mind?" she said, "Sweet Jesus, you are a total nutter."

"Why, Brigid, why?" I am getting angry now. I met Liam in the moment, and he stood up to the mark. He had signed on the dotted line. He had given me his vow.

"Because Fiona is pregnant you poor sad cow."

PART THREE

Chapter One

It is Bob who comes up with a plan. He is warrior again, worrier again. He has a friend who has a house in New Haven in County Wexford. It is a holiday place and very primitive, but it is free over the winter. He rings his friend, who argues with him. It turns out my stepmum is on the warpath. Bob grimaces at me and leaves the room to continue the conversation. When he returns he explains that he has told his friend everything. But his friend will not tell his mother. His friend has agreed to give Bob the key and not turn him in.

Brigid is not keen on the plan, but reluctantly she agrees it is a plan.

"That is a new thing for you Bella," she says, shaking her head but her eyebrows mercifully down. In place and where they should be. "It has the makings of a plan and may give you time to think."

I nod sagely and then curse savagely when I discover my phone is missing and will not return to its rightful owner. I am still tearing down my room, tearing out my hair, tearing a new one, when Brigid walks in with a replacement.

"You are not going far," she says. "But smoke signals will not work between counties. Use this, it's Mick's and he won't miss it. Never bloody thinks to use it anyway."

I'm not that hopeful but I need out of here. There is no shelter for me. I feel, oddly, like Mary. Suddenly pregnant, suddenly in shame, suddenly without a father and Bob will do a Joseph for me. I always wondered what Joseph thought, especially in those days. Take on a woman with child, in a part of the world and a time of the world, where her crime was of greater value than the joint lives of her and her unborn child. It still happens and for fucks sake, it happened here until the Pope visited, not that he had anything to do with changing that, but no one ever asked how Joseph felt.

Or maybe they did. Maybe his mother asked him earnestly if he was sure he wanted to take on … that slut? That fallen woman? That poor creature? History does not record what she felt and thought. And what about his father? Did he box him one?

"You stupid idiot, you cuckhold, you prickhead!" he roared at Joseph. "You want to bring shame on our family then you can fuck out of here. I'm not giving you the family furniture business, that goes to Roger. You can fuck off you effeminate pansy!"

I'm not sure but it can't have been good, I'd say. I see Joseph's father heading out for a drink with lads. He is sick and tired of his wife's crying and lamenting. Joseph has always been his mother's favourite. He is the one who stays home and discusses interiors with her. While the father and brothers all make big functional furniture, stuff you can lay a bull out on, slay a virgin on, feed a family on, Joseph has always been the artistic one, creating delicate tables, tall boys, intricately carved occasional tables.

"I mean," Joseph's father bemoans to his friends in the bar, "just what the fuck is an occasional table? It either is a table or it's fucking not!"

His friends, all clutching large earthen ware jugs of whatever the fuck they drink in those times, all agree, shaking their heads and spitting violently onto the floor. It's possibly only the fact the Joseph's father is such a big mean fucker that they haven't already kicked three bells of shit out of Joseph. Some, behind his back, quietly say maybe it's not such a bad thing. Who else would have him anyway?

Joseph's mother watches her husband go to the pub. She knows exactly what he is thinking. She has spent her life as a buffer between Joseph and his father. His three sturdy brothers are equally intolerant, but they don't care. He is only their brother after all and not the fruit of their loins. They don't give a fuck as long as he stays away from them and to be honest, they quite like how he has decorated the main house, not that they'd ever say it, but God help their wives for they won't be able to maintain them in style quite as Joseph did.

How did Joseph's mother manage to produce such a quiet, gentle soul? From that brute of a husband and just watch the other boys. Even her one daughter Helena has more testosterone than Joseph. Of course, the answer is easy and guess what, history is repeating itself, after a fashion.

Joseph is the last son, the last child. That possibly spared him from sibling fratricide. For ten years Joseph's mother was a wife and mother. For ten minutes she was a woman who lay with another man. She should have been more sympathetic to Mary, you'd think? Except, Mary was messing with her beloved son, destroying his life. Anyone who did that was in for trouble, period. But also, this whole fucking virginal birth was giving her the gripe. She, more than anyone, understood the temptation and ultimately the penalty to be paid for ten minutes of sin. But the fucking Mary had not sinned according to Joseph. This was tearing his mother apart.

"The little whore, the trollop, the slut," she said through clenched teeth. She could not say this to Joseph for she could bear anything other than losing him. How little she understood the power of religion. She could not say anything to anyone for fear of showing her hand. Then it would be her and also Joseph down the tube. And she'd fought so hard for his existence, to bring him as a man to the world. Her blood was in his veins. Just her's. For this too was her virgin birth. Her awesome delivery to mankind. But, she didn't realise that she just was the rehearsal and her son, the stool pigeon. What mother could wish for that?

Chapter Two

Bob opens the door and George bounds in first. Despite some well-meaning but utterly ineffectual obedience training by Brigid, George remains hopelessly out of control. He enters doors first, no gentleman George, because he believes he is the leader of the pack. He leads in the kitchen, in the living room, which is an exercise in mounting futility because the little shit does not know where I am going. I often kick him out of the way, not playfully, as he impedes yet another journey across the kitchen or to the living room.

"You don't know where I am going George so just don't bother," I yell at him. He remains silent but is, I can see, affronted. To put me in my place, he just raises a baleful eye to me, a look that I am wholly immune to, but he hasn't figured this out yet. Let him stew!

This time it is Bob who curses as George bounds in, and then suddenly remembers there is a member of his tribe waiting for guidance. Accordingly, he bounds back to pick up the leading position, only to knock against Bob's legs and cause him to stumble step into the bungalow.

"Fuck off George," shouts Bob, and George, happy to be of assistance, continues to lead Bob through the house. Tag wagging. It's a dog's life.

The bungalow is tiny and very plain and smells of damp. Not unpleasantly, but the smell familiar to all holiday houses, only really used in the summer, locked up in the damp months and with no central heating. There are two bedrooms, an open-plan kitchen, a living room and a shared bathroom with separate toilet. That's it, except when I look at the kitchen door, I am surprised. A long American style veranda runs the length of the back wall. It wasn't visible when we drove in the front. It is jerry built but covered in a climbing rambler, half dead now but bushy enough to render it rustic. There is even an obligatory rocking chair.

I unlock the three sets of bolts that stop the criminals from entering and ransacking this priceless home. The bolts seem almost apologetic and slide back with ease. A good kick from the outside would dislodge all three in a single blow. Or maybe, I think, it's to stop great uncle Frederick from sleepwalking over the cliff. But there is no great uncle and no cliff, just a veranda that is charming, for all its wonkiness. Bob is beside me.

"Oh, I like this," he says, diving past me and plonking himself onto the rocking chair. "Dibbs on this seat," he says cheekily. I look round and the only other seating available is a faded and misshapen green plastic chair.

"Oi, pregnant women get first dibbs on rocking chairs," I tell him, and he moves laughing.

For the first time in a long time, I feel happy. I've solved nothing but I made a plan and this time it worked. For the moment anyway. That night Bob and I play cards. We have no choice. Neither of us is drinking, he's not that bothered and I'm faintly nauseous when it comes to alcohol. The television is tiny and limited to local stations. There is an American cop show on RTE2, the news on RTE1, some stupid reality programme on TV3 and absolute crap on

TnaG, or at least it looks crap but since neither of us can speak Irish, we're only guessing.

A search round the house has not turned up many treasures. A couple of very old folding chairs, buckets and spades for forgotten children, a tatty beach umbrella, battered board games of the big-name variety, missing most of their pieces and cards, four packs of cards. We decide on a card night. We start with poker, which is in fact one of the most boring games ever invented. And there is, after all, only the two of us. So, we move to Snap, very entertaining, Rummy, interesting, Cheat, hilarious, 45, stimulating and 105, mind boggling.

"Enough," I cry after two hours of intense gaming.

I move to the window. The night is cold and cloudless. It is not late, but it's not early either. Not drinking does funny things to my nighttime activities. Everything finishes earlier, except maybe for tanked up lovers. I'm slightly restless but also very tired.

"Let's call it a day," I suggest. I haven't asked Bob how long he can stay or what he plans on doing next. One plan at a time. The current plan, which is sort of hovering on its expiry date, its sell by date, was to move here. I, we have done that. The bags are unpacked, beds made, milk in the fridge. We are ensconced in a bungalow, ugly but with a charming American veranda. Or perhaps we are staying in a charming American veranda that happens to be attached to a rather ugly, if functional, bungalow. Yes, I think I like that better.

"Where are you living now Bella?"

"Oh, in a charming American veranda. It's a little run down, you know, but very sweet. Covered in a bushy, non-specific rambler. Or rather, it very probably is specific, just not to me. And it's dark, so I can't really see it. But what was I saying, yes, my veranda, so sweet. So simple but I call it home. And the best bit is that it also boasts an ensuite bungalow, very handy for sleeping and other functional stuff like going to the loo or cooking dinner, very handy."

"An interesting home you say? Yes, indeed. Pared back to the basics, my dear. Very green, very noughties, very avant garde."

"You know me, darling, always in the mode."

And for once, I don't finish by cursing my little veranda home. It is sweet. I do believe my soliloquy. I do, I believe I'm going to enjoy my veranda. It sure beats a stable and I'm not sharing with any ruminating animals.

"'Night Bob, and thanks."

Chapter Three

New Haven is a one-horse town. I thought Ballybawn small,
but New Haven is only a linear development. There is a
ribbon of brightly coloured houses that begins with the speed
limits and a ramp, and ends with 'end of speed limits' signs,
and another ramp. In between there is a petrol pump, a pub
and a garage forecourt, with tyres lined up in double rows like
sentinels. I walk into the pub with Bob, and we are given the
silent treatment, which is to say, the barman is very polite and
attentive and everyone else watches us over the rim of their
glasses. It is home from home. Thursday night and the pub is
not busy, but then it is only nine o'clock. Niall, the barman,
asks if we are local.

"Yes," I tell him, "we're the new locals." But he won't
make much out of us, given that I am drinking orange juice
and Bob is nursing a single pint, he is driving he says and
refuses to have another.

This minding of me is not meant to be so serious. I
look at Bob and try to figure him out. He looks back at me
and does the same. We both give up. It must be a family
thing. A shared genetic laziness, that or genuine
unfathomability. Naturally, we both prefer the latter, but I
think it may be laziness really. We are skirting round issues,
talking pure rubbish, having fun it must be said. This
relationship with Bob is really easy, really lazy. He is blood
but there is no angst. How can it be so different I wonder. I
trust him. Plain and simple. I also don't expect anything of

him. This is a wonderful feeling. Again, I am happy. And it's a joy that does not rely on drugs, sex or money. How weird is that? Because I expect nothing and just feel, it's like being cushioned on air, walking on mattresses, bubbling through water. Bob at this stage tells me I am mad.

"I know," I agree. I am mad enough to begin a plan. Another one. Fuck, there is bravery or confidence or both. One plan followed by another. Wow – I must be doing something right. Or maybe just doing something.

So, after much considered discussion the plan is as follows. I will get a job, 'possibly in this pub' I gesture airily, expansively around. Then I will get a man. I have written off the other fathers and unlike my once pregnant, out of wedlock, colleague in arms, babe in arms, I cannot rely on divine intervention. I mean, I can try, but in my newly sober form, I genuinely don't think it a good plan, and don't regard it as an option at all.

"Thank the fuck," breathes Bob.

Which brings me onto my next problem. How shall I find a man? In this tiny village, this main street, this inconspicuous, inoffensive little hamlet? The internet of course. I am quite excited at this point, but Bob is starting to look pained.

"It is alright," I stress as if to a child of small understanding. "It is quite normal to seek romance over the net, really."

What is the third part of my plan? I don't think there is one, but since I always think in trinities, there should be one, or rather there should be three. Job, Man…baby maybe?

I've decided to go for the meat in the sandwich first, of course. What else would you expect? So I am describing myself as engaging, fun loving, bright, interesting. "Are you mentioning pregnant?" asks Bob unhelpfully.

"Fuck no," I say. "Do you think I want to scare them off from the get go. I need to be a bit subtle here."

Of course, subtlety is not my forte. Nor Bob's, there's a surprise and another family resemblance.

"Say you have big tits," he says.

"I don't," I mention quite reasonably for me. "They are beautiful but not big."

"Doesn't matter," Bob says. "They will be soon." He has a point.

So, I am a big breasted woman looking for a man. How hard can it be? When I say this to Bob he cracks up and so do I. I send off my details and wait.

And wait. Fuck, I'm very bad at waiting.

Chapter Four

I have four emails and two winks waiting for me in the morning. It seems that men like big breasted fun-loving women, go figure? Or maybe it was the bit I added at the end, that 'I liked being naughty.' A killer ad if you ask me. Eagerly I open the mails. The first, from Strongbow, is good. No picture, but then neither had I, and Strongbow wants to know more about me, why am I seeking romance online, what I enjoy doing in my spare time, what size are my tits?

I laugh out loud and look down. Are they bigger already perhaps? Should I give an interim size or the end size expected? I decide to go for maximum impact, after all I need to find a man sooner rather than later and tell him 36DD. To give an idea of my exaggeration, I'm a more modest 36C. I like the sound of Strongbow. I like the image his name conjures up. Images captured on the back of my retina when a child and visiting Christchurch cathedral in Dublin. I think I may have caught a rare school trip there, but I know I went back again when not in school, playing truant, and perhaps once with mother. I'm not sure why she went there, it is a protestant cathedral after all and she was, is very catholic, very roman catholic.

The large tomb of Strongbow always fascinated me, knight laid out and vast, huge, imposing in death as perhaps only death can really impose. I ran my fingers on the edge of his stone effigy. It felt as though he could rise up, rise up and give orders, bark them out in the echoing waves that filled the cathedral. People talking at the entrance could be heard as muffled ripples that chased each other round the walls. The sound then jelly-belied up to the arched ceilings, vibrated a bit in the grey air, before falling softly like spent snowflakes onto the pews. Imagine all the prayers vibrating across the cathedral, did they ever escape, escape up to God, or just quiver in the still dusty air. Falling only when the energy was spent. Did fervent prayers last longer, linger longer? What did Strongbow think listening to all these conversations with God? Was he tired of them, pissed off at the endless repetition of requests for health, for wealth, for sons to get jobs, daughters to get sons, mothers to heal relations, fathers to cope with the daily, weekly slavery to life?

After all, Strongbow was not God, not an immortal, all seeing, all understanding being. Strongbow was just a conqueror laid to rest in a cathedral. What did he care of the petty worries of plebs? Perhaps this was his eternal punishment for his warlording. Listen always to the little people. Hear the constant prayers of the people. Oh, how they must weary the non-gods. How they must weary the gods, the God. Is there no relief? Please help my son. Rescue my Sean. Help my Karen. We have no money to pay the heating. I hate my husband; I want to leave him. Help me be a better person lord. Hands together in supplication. Heads bowed. Prayers littering the floor like confetti blowing outside the church. Only now, confetti is banned, so if you must throw something, use rose petals. Throw prayers, throw prayers at Strongbow's feet, and let him chaff, always tuned in to the endless, mindless twitter of prayers.

All looped and rolled into circles. And interspersed with chores and idle stray thoughts. Did I turn off the iron?

Dear lord, please help my son with his exams. Must buy bread on the way home, look at that girl's hair, please forgive me lord for I have sinned. I am a sinner, and I repent me, repent me, God that hair is just terrible. A bird's nest, so messy, did it ever see a comb, thanks be to God. Oh, the litany goes on and on.

"Shut up you fuckers" roars Strongbow. "You're doing my fucking head in. Shut the fuck up will you!"

The other mails and winks do not move me. I am captured by Strongbow. I see him in my mind's eye. He is six foot plus. He is solid and clothed in armour. He is a leader of men. He asks me for my mobile. Pretty forward I think but then he is a leader of men, I must obey. Strongbow is strong and he will carry me to happiness. He is online now, his star winks. I text him my number. My mobile beeps. That was fast, but he is a leader of men and is confident.

"Hi babe," he writes. "I'm very happy to meet u". Another beep and a picture arrives on my phone. "Oh Strongbow," I think. "You don't beat around the bush." No, but he is beating his meat.

A picture of him holding his erect penis flashes on my phone. Then another bleep and a video arrives. This time, he is wanking his cock on my phone. I watch, and he comes. I do not think this video is from this morning. I suspect it has been filmed prior and sent to more than just me. I stop and I contemplate this video. How do I feel about Strongbow now and his picture and video? This is a very good question. As I contemplate, another bleep and another video. This time it is Strongbow fucking a woman from behind. This image is grainy and up close. All I can see is his cock entering her pussy. He is wearing a condom which looks strangely incongruous in this video. I didn't think Strongbow would have had access to condoms. I see his armour but not latex armour. I am distracted when Bob walks into the room, sleep headed.

I show him my new friend's videos, and he practically explodes with anger.

"What the fuck are you doing Bella," he shouts. "Why did you give that creep your number?"

I just laugh. "I think he is looking for his next co-star," I suggest. "Anyway, it is Mick's phone so let Strongbow worry when a big hairy biker comes to visit him." I start to laugh very hard now and even Bob sees the funny side.

"God help Mick," he says walking off. "He'll have to go to therapy for years after this…"

And so, Bob has had enough of sex texts and videos. He goes to the bathroom with a paper. Gosh, he is feeling at home here! Another beep. This time a video of Strongbow and a headless woman giving him a hand job. On this video there is plenty of sound, from Strongbow. He is breathing very heavily. He calls her a sexy bitch, a fucking whore. The headless woman says nothing. One hand is pushing down on his belly, and even in the tight angle and the lying down position, it looks a rather large belly, the other works on Strongbow's cock.

She has a French polish I notice. I wonder did she have it done for the date or did she know she was going to be filmed. On and on she wanks him. It is only for seconds but watching her hands, her tits squished between her arms, his cock pulled up and down, and the image is strangely etched on my retina, again. Finally, he comes. He spurts up crazily, then slops over her hand and her French polish, it is noisy and wet. He groans with pleasure, loudly. And the headless woman says nothing.

Strongbow sends me another communication. I can only think he is not busy this morning.   "Send me some videos of you, babe" he implores.

Later I thank him for his offerings but decline to reciprocate. He asks several more times and I still refuse. Finally, Strongbow tells me that he is not interested in meeting me unless he can see the goods first.

I am disappointed at Strongbow. I had expected more of him. Just goes to show that prayer is not always the answer.

Chapter Five

Brigid is amused. So is Bob, if a little worried. Minding his big sister is not quite the wholesome, hole some, holy pastime he first envisioned. I don't think he had a vision, really. More of a vocation and we all know how they can turn out.

"What do you mean?" asks Brigid.

Bob is not in my little veranda cum bungalow. He has gone for a walk in the fresh air. I think maybe he has walked to the pub. It is not far. I don't blame him. He is minding mother and child, and I am messing about. Looking for sex is not really the same as looking for a man. I'm not sure what I am doing, really. Passing the time, maybe.

"Passing wind for sure," says Brigid. Passing the port if I could. Or passing for a good person? Passing the buck. Stopping for fuck. Not passing the fuck. "Not passing away either," says Brigid.

"It's a bit hard for a corpse to pass wind," I remark.

"Not really," shoots back Brigid. "All those gasses escaping the body. It's a constant exhalation. Like breathing but foul gas instead of air. And none going back in again of course. The wind escapes and the body falls in on itself. Passing on you might say."

"Passing on the fuck awful characteristics to the next generation, more like," I shout.

I'm not sure why I am shouting. Except it feels good.
Feels like I should shout. Brigid jerks back as my air, my
wind, as it passes from my mouth in a gust. It's like when you
blow on a dog's face. She jerks, then blinks. Blinks again. It's
not like I've done anything on purpose, but the sudden shout
is a blow. A blow of air. Innocuous until you consider great
winds, the mistral, the fohn, all rushing down a valley and
pulling at things. At bits of houses that are not secure. At
garden objects not tied down. Rubbish bins lined at the back
of the streets, some tipped over and debris sprawling in the
gusts. Eddies of papers and plastic cups lift in swirls, before
tumbling into new corners, always just out of reach, should
you wish to catch them. Quick, put your foot down on it.
Stamp on it, no, there it goes again, just out of reach. Bugger
it!

We make dinner. Bob does not return. I text him but
there is no answer. Brigid has brought the dinner with her. I
guess she knew my limited ability and suspected, rightly,
Bob's.

"It is," I tell her fondly, "cupboard love a thing with
me, a very fine dinner. Stuffed chicken breasts, asparagus tips
sauteed in butter, new potatoes."

We put Bob's dinner in the oven, covered
with a plate.

"He may eat it when he returns," I say.

"Or I may eat it before he returns. Or for breakfast."
Brigid pulls a face.

We are pulled inexorably back to the dating site.
There are a number of emails flashing at me. One is from

HLAD. We wonder what it stands for. There is no picture, but he seems interesting. Tall, blonde, own house, car, good job, loves women, very sensitive, caring lover.

The list is like a "how to make a perfect man."

We send him a wink. Quick as a flash, one comes back.

"Oh, he's online," I say.

"Send an email, then," suggests Brigid.

I look at her for a moment and then type "how u? wot do u luk lik?"

The site is not that fast, or else he is holding multiple conversations.

Finally, after what seems like an interminable period, he writes back, "I'm told I'm handsome. U wana chat some? Go messaging?"

Why not? In a few more emails, where contacts are swapped, I move to my gmail account. The window opens and HLAD is online too.

"So ure handsome?" I ask again

"Yeah, and broad"

"Broad?"

"Broadminded…ru?"

"Depends…."

"ru on site 4sex or friendship ??"

"Both maybe"

"r u horny now?" Boy, he moves fast and I gesture to Brigid to come join me at the pc. I grin at her. Together we watch his blinking answers

"wot does HLAD mean? Handsome lad?"

"hung like a donkey"

"r u?"

"of course. Want 2c? u got videocam?"

Fuck. I look at Brigid.

"Of course I don't here. Mind you, we don't want a videocam here," she says. "I've no intention of flashing him anything. But he has, so maybe we can load up the software."

I giggle. This is fun. I start the download in the background.

"do u like cock?"

"not really. Do u?"

"y don't u lik it?"

I look at Brigid. We are laughing now.

"Cos im a lesbian."

"r u alone?"

"no, my partner is with me."

"wot u doin? Fingerin each other?"

We laugh a little harder now. What shall we answer?

"No, we are doing the crossword" We splurt with laughter now. I quickly type some more.

"We're stuck on four across." I pause for a bit trying to rack my brains for a clue. Fuck.

"What is the longitude of fiji?" I type. Brigid lets out a howl of laughter. "What on earth are you on about? What kind of clue is that? Fuck knows, but it doesn't put HLAD off his stride."

"id like to get stuck in2 both of u," appears on the screen and then a moment later, "r u wet now?"

I think for a moment. Brigid is still laughing at the crossword joke. "Oh," she says, "say we are eco warriors." And I do. Moreover, I state that since we are committed eco warriors we conserve water. We rarely shower, maybe once a week and then together of course. We haven't showered so far this week, so we are therefore very dry.

Brigid and I are in convulsions at this point. HLAD is not one to give up easily. He sends us another invitation to view his webcam, but I notice the download has failed. Poxy thing.

"We are very hairy women," I add for good measure.

"hairy pussys?"

"no cats, only dogs. And a goldfish"

"A what?" squeaks Brigid. "What are two eco warriors doing with a goldfish? We don't have enough water for a goldfish!"

"goldfish dying cos of lack of water, very sad."

"ur two sad lessers"

"it was fun, tho"

"yeah, I lafted"

"see ya donkey!"

"What ever"

We are still laughing when Bob comes back in from the pub, slightly drunk, just enough to be cross at the goldfish. Just enough to be amused by it too. I hadn't eaten his dinner so that cheers him up too.

This internet dating is good fun. I can't wait for more. What else is blowing in the wind? Fuck knows. Flotsam and jetsam. Flotsam and jetsam. Just not the answer, I know that.

Chapter Six

Contender number three is much more promising. For
starters he has resisted all sextalk, sexting, or sexmailing. He
is, it appears, normal. We begin corresponding while Brigid is
still with me, and continue on afterwards. Brigid can only stay
three days. It is a good time, and we enjoy the laughter. She
asks me what I am going to do and I can't answer her.
Because I do not know. Really. On her last morning, she
crawls into bed with me. We hold each other. She strokes my
belly.

"What is growing here?" she asks.

"Who is growing here?" I reply.

"Who indeed," she says. We are silent, like a couple. I
listen to her breathing. There are very few constants in my
life.

"I want you to be with me for this child," I say
quietly. "For the birth and after. Will you be there?"

Brigid nods her head. She pats my belly, my unborn
sprog. "Wild horses wouldn't stop me."

I feel tears welling up inside me. Big, splashy tears.
"Good, I just wanted to know."

"History won't repeat itself," she says quietly. "You
are who you are. Your child will be. Maybe though you
should connect back with your mother. If you want to

understand who you are. She will be a grandmother soon enough too."

"If she lives that long."

"Yeah, there is that. She is not well, at all."

"I know."

Contender number three is very quirky. He wears a beanie hat. He is a carpenter. He plays in a band. He lives by himself with two dogs. He has four brothers, all married and with children whom he really enjoys. He is very busy. He works long hours at his work; he is with a busy construction firm that is part of a development consortium. He plays five a side football twice a week, practices with his bluegrass band once a week, drinks to excess at least one night of the weekend, goes to Sunday lunch with his mum. He has had lots of girlfriends. The last one painted her nails black and dyed her pubes purple. They split because she disliked his music, which he found ironic since he didn't like hers at all.

"Still," he said, all waving arms. "She was great in the sack and a super cook and a real bird, lovely!" he almost smacked his lips but pulled himself up at the last moment. We have arranged a meeting in a hotel. He has taken a room here. Peter, his name, is being very, well Peter. He is interesting, very honest, straight to the point. He lives some two hours drive away and staying makes sense. I am thirty minutes from here and am not drinking of course. I am keeping my own counsel. We have corresponded for three weeks.

We progressed from email to texting to talking. He has a nice way with words. He is caring. He is also increasingly cheeky and sexy. It is bizarre. All my previous lovers have been from the sex get go. Now, I am internet dating and pregnant, not that I have told him or anyone on the site for that matter, I have started from the non sex and am working forward. He has been very gentlemanly. It is so different, I am totally flummoxed. But when we meet in the flesh he is suddenly galvanised into sex. It is so funny. First, I hear about his ex-girl friends' peccadilloes which is somewhat off putting. Then he starts to tell me about his own.

He is a big fan of spanking, which I have to say turns me on. But I make the mistake of asking him an intellectual question on this subject.

"Do you actually like giving pain?," I ask. And next I am flooded with an enthusiasm for spanking that leaves the Jesuits for dust. And there is wax mentioned, hot wax and skin. Thank you but I have had enough bikini waxing to leave this little pleasure behind. I wonder is this a deal breaker but no, Peter relaxes again. I think nerves are in play.

By his third pint, Peter is considerably more mellow. We are synching now. Conversation has reached a pattern understood by both of us. He talks, I listen. I talk, he listens. We blend in and out of our conversations in a comfortable way. I am enjoying his company. He leans over me again, and to stress a point, slaps my leg. He looks at me and his eyes dance. He stands and takes me in his arms. He swings me round, then faster. The music is very loud. The bed is behind me and he pushes me onto it.

I fall back, mattress cutting my knees and jack knifing me clumsily horizontal. He pushes me over and my bare rump is exposed in the air. He is spanking me, hard. Then the hand changes to a crop and there are welts. Tears are in my eyes. The pain is intense, like a wall. My eyes are blurred with pain. I cannot see. My tears fall like hot wax down my cheeks. It is relentless and I feel no relief. Peter is standing over me, whip in hand, no phallus in hand. I feel no relief, no escape, no pleasure. I do not even feel his. Instead, I stand up. In my haste I almost knock over the end of my drink. Peter looks at me questioningly.

"What's the matter, hun?" he says. "Cold feet?"

"Er, I'm pregnant," I splurt out.

And exit stage right.

Chapter Seven

Maybe it is time to go back to Ballybawn. I debate this with Bob who has returned. It reminds me of a suicide watch. Brigid and Bob are taking it in turns to watch me. I weigh up the pros. And cons.

"You need something to do," says Bob. "Right now, you're just waiting for Godot."

Godot didn't show up, go figure, so instead I persuade Niall in the pub, the aptly named

"Corner House" to give me a job.

I say aptly named, for I am cleaning. Cleaning the Pooh at the house in the Corner. How can country drinkers make such a mess I wonder. At ten o'clock I am there, mop in hand like a seventies advert. I wash the bar, cleaning the sticky surfaces. The floor is wood but dusty wood. Dogs are allowed in. If I pat the cushions on the bar stools, great big clouds of dust rise up in the early morning sunlight. I feel as if I am just moving the dust around. From bar to floor. From stools to floor. Then I sweep the floor and the dust swirls up and settles onto the bar. I mop the floor and at least that moves the dust out, chemically captured by the water, I think. Bonded. H_2O and dust equals sludge.

Lovely, I think as I then have to really push the mop in front of me. This is hard work but not compared to the toilets.

If men claim to be able to park, why can't they aim straight in the urinal? The stench is awful and yet I am sure there could not have been more than twelve men in the pub the previous night. This is New Haven for fucks sake. And how come there are always shit marks on the side of the toilets? Do the locals come here to shit?

I feel I am marking time. Marking time. I swish and I mop.

Paddy, a retired farmer (can farmers retire?) is here most mornings. His terrier Brad (I kid you not) is old and incontinent. He tends to wee uncontrollably when patted. I dread when visitors arrive and innocently pat his head, while talking with old Paddy. Paddy himself is full of talk, always the same talk, the same conversation, but delivered with enthusiasm each time. The same conversation is new each time, which is cool if you are a visitor looking for local interest but boring as shite for me and possibly the other regulars, but I'm not sure about that as they too have the exact same conversations even if they are ten years younger and not yet the owner of an incontinent dog.

To be fair to Paddy, he is a gentleman. When the tourists go and Brad's piss, and God help us, sometimes shit, is pointed out, he will with fervour curse the poor God forsaken tourist that was the cause of the unletting.

"The fucking cunt," he apologies to me, "if I had known he was petting Brad I would have given him a piece of my fucking mind. Who did he think he was, the stupid eejit." And he will make a great show of shaking his fist at the long departed tourist, and then of moving his stool, and drink, and incontinent fucking terrier up the bar.

Paddy of course is not incontinent, but I suspect he may be responsible for some of the crap I have to clean up in the men's toilets. I can only surmise of course, since I do not follow him in or spy on him. I like Paddy, hate his fucking miserable excuse of a dog, and only biding time on this job. There is a time limit on this for sure.

As for the women's toilets. As for. Actually, they are fine. The average age of the women who drink here is mid-fifties or sixties. They do not get drunk, or at least not the drunk of kids. I only ever cleaned up puke once, and then from Maree Toner who, allegedly, had seven pints of Carlsberg, two whiskeys and a Baileys. I'd say it was the Baileys that did it. The creamy puke washed down one wall. I think she must have projectile vomited across the cubicle. It was pure Baileys in colour though sick smells, sick regardless of race, colour and creed. Shit must be the same too I reckon, though in the women's toilet there was never any evidence. I put that down to women not shitting full stop. At least not in public. Whom am I kidding!

Chapter Eight

There is no warning. Nothing. Before there is dull quiet and even with a tsunami or an earthquake there is supposed to be a seismic rumble or a prescient quiet. An expectant pause. Into which something gives birth. Sometimes it is a subtraction rather than an addition though, a removal of life and not an arrival. Or can death be called a birth? Who knows unless you are the recipient and enter a new way. Many talk of near death and the white light waiting. Some have said that it is the birth canal and the opening of the second womb, second life, regeneration. I surely do not the fuck know.

No warning. I am cleaning piss and shite and the debris of drinking life. I am walking the dog. I am talking with Bob. I am sitting on my American Veranda. I am enjoying the good life, well a life, and I am treading water. Having been blindsided with multiple pregnancies, of which mine is only one, I am just hanging in there and okay with this. I am formulating. At some stage it will become a plan. I do know it.

And while I am formulating and waiting, and planning which the gods hate, and thinking through my options, wading through my thoughts, weighing up my prospectives, while I still think I have a choice, the fucking gods pull the carpet from under my feet. You have to understand, I didn't own the carpet in the first place, but I was standing there, so did I not have squatters' rights? Did the 'vote with your feet' not have any pull? Did the 'give the fucking girl a fucking break' not come into play? Fuck me, my life has been so far bereft of fair play, but still, I like to have had a choice.

Chapter Nine

Bridge claims second victim. Aqueduct. Aqueduct. It's a fucking aqueduct. That's what claimed him. Not a fucking bridge. An aqueduct carries water. Bridges go places. They go over troubled water. Like a.

He was falling. Falling like a stone. He was falling apart. Falling asunder. Falling in love. No, he fell in love a long time ago. He was falling out of love. Into despair. Dis repair. No repair.

He fell. His body fell. Mortal pulp, smashed. His face went backwards through his head. Or so they said. The coffin closed. The limbs all bent back into place; missing curves, flattened, splattened, unshaped, unmade, unlaid. Laid to rest in pieces. Laid to rest in peace.

I do not go inside the church. I can not go inside the church. I wait outside. There are many people anyway. The church is full. Full from early. People come and sign the book at the door and then shuffle off to one side. Talk in low voices. Waiting, watching, talking in low voices.

The rain holds off, thank God, says my neighbour. I look at him, through him and away from him. What the fuck does the weather have to do with the anything?

Rain doesn't matter anymore to Liam.

I watch them bring out the coffin from the church and carry it to the graveside. The crowds are legend. His mother is there, weeping, and inconsolable. His father is there, tight faced and angry. Fiona and her swelling belly too of course. The crowds crowd round the open maw of the grave. Pitch him in. pitch him in. Stare too long into the hole and it sucks you in.

The priest intones and assembled parishioners echo back to him. Waves of prayer flow in and out, incantations rise up and down. Heads bowed and hands clasped in front, occasionally a sob breaks out, or a whimper. A number of small children play oblivious to the tragedy, play at the edge of the grave, voices low but smiles darting across their faces as they scamper backwards and forwards.

I watch them and block out the prayers, the chanting. I let the communal prayer wash over me as a blessing. Slide across me and down onto the grass where the noise quivers in the morning air before disappearing into the soil. Soaked in and sucked up. Prayer is gone into the ground ahead of Liam, to prepare a way for Liam. He is still cocooned in the coffin, still sheltered from the soil, the damp, the roots, the worms. I watch the prayer settle and soak in. Sometimes it bounces a little, like an overgrown bubble, before ping! It bursts and the droplets soak away. As I watch I wander. The prayers have stopped now; we have reached the end of the formal grieving. I wander lonely as a cloud. That floats on high o're hill and vale. And all at once I see a crowd, a crowd out to lynch me. My wandering has taken me too close to the grave. I am in the queue of people shaking hands and whispering condolences. I do not mean to be here. I have followed the surge and now I am poised in front of the equally pregnant Fiona who recoils from me as if I am poisonous, which I may be. I don't know. Maybe I am deadly nightshade, maybe I will infect her. She has pulled back her hand like a tortoise recoiling into its shell. The look of horror is palpable on her eyes. And then it moves from horror to anger, vivid as a blush covering her face. She pulls, clutches, pecks ineffectually at Liam's mother who is engrossed in a conversation next to her.

"You," is all she can spit out.

Her almost, mother-in-law is not so tongue tied. She is quite loquacious, truth be told. She turns from her engrossed conversation and her eyes alight on me. Light up me. It is like a beacon turning to me, a lighthouse light sweeping across the vista but stopping suddenly and focusing only on me. I know I like to be the centre of attention, but this is ridiculous. And so is she. To think that I had picked her son to be the father of my unborn child, perish the thought. Are all mothers the same I wonder? Her venom is such that she spits her words on me. I am drenched in her spittle and bile. This is not prayer; this is the antithesis of prayer. If prayer can bounce and ping, this diatribe can only drop and sting. She reaches deep into her gut to express the utter loathing she has grown for me.

I do not want this mother to be grandmother to my child. Fuck, I do not want my own mother to be grandmother to my unborn child. Is my unborn child to be grandmotherless?. How sad, a child not yet born and already I am discarding key relatives with summary abandonment. To lose one grandparent is unfortunate, two, reeks of irresponsibility. And this is not comedy, we are too wide off that mark, too damn Wilde.

I am about to answer back. To retract the grandmotherness. There, you only have one unborn child to spoil. But Fiona finds the wind beneath her wings, encouraged no doubt by the hot air of abuse coming from almost mother-in-law. She is buoyed up on the hot air current. Egged on by the fish wife venom of almost mother-in- law.

"Don't you dare to pretend to be carrying Liam's child," she spits. "You open your legs for any tom, dick or harry. You don't even know who the father is. It wasn't Liam. He told me he hadn't been with you in months."

Mother-in-law practically ignites at this stage.

"You fucking bitch," she screams. "You called him, didn't you? Told him you were pregnant, and you threatened him. He knew it wasn't his child, but you tried to blackmail him. Why else did he go to the bridge? Why else did he jump?"

Suddenly there is silence. The wind drops and the squall is spent. Everyone has stopped and everyone is listening. A pin could drop and it would be heard. Why do the events of my life turn on the falling of a pin? Why are they always while the cameras are turning, the world watching, the media listening? I empathise with the children of celebrities. I know the god-awful feeling of the world watching your next step, the next mistake, your next fuckup.

"What do you mean?" I ask. "I did not call him for at least two months."

"You called him the night he died."

Chapter Ten

Have you ever fed a lover with just your hands? Closed your eyes and trusted, just trusted?

Brigid and I are holding hands. We are walking on the beach. I am shaking, but it is not just the cold wind. The walk before the run. I am cold to my core. I cannot feel my core.

"Enough," she declares and pulls me back to the car. "We are going home."

It's only half past the point of oblivion, Mick's mobile is on the table, and we look at it as if there is meaning. It is the breath before the kiss, and the fear before the flames. Have you ever felt this way?

You called me Babe. I called him Babe. But I never called him that night.

It's only half past the point of no return.

Chapter Eleven

For once I am nonplussed. I stroke my belly and cogitate.
Those crazy thoughts are travelling round my head. They
stem from my belly. My belly is bigger now, formed now,
active now. My unborn child is screaming for revenge. Asking
the questions. Posing ten different answers, of which all ten
may be totally wrong, or one may be right. It is a dangerous
occupation, posing questions to which no one knows the
answer and then answering them, one by one, and as a result
having the additional skills of a gifted multiplier.

One plus one equals four. I may be nonplussed, but I
am plussing with the abandon of an alcoholic at a free bar.
Just one tipple here, oh, go on then, add another. What?
Whiskey chaser, yes please. And perhaps a glass of bubbly to
celebrate and a glass of stout for strength. And that new cider
looks lovely in its long neck bottle, oh yes please to a nice
g&t. Knock them back, drink them down. Sing the song, pat
the back of the barman, hardworking barman and soon my
eyes are doubling up. Is this a dagger which I see before me?
Or is it two? Which is more real: the vision or reality? Which
is more real to me? If I see two, does it make it so? Is truth
always the accumulation of answers or is it the multiplication
of them? Is my truth different to yours? And does it matter to
whom I compare my truths? Come let me clutch thee, and
perhaps then I can see you still.

Of course, there is at least one person who knows the
answer and he is dead, deep buried in the silent tomb. He

cannot rise up and oppose my sea of fucking troubles. He cannot begin to comprehend them, being dead. But then he was pretty useless while alive. Am I getting bitter already? Quite possibly. In life, the sum of his happiness quite outpaced mine. His sums were of the singular kind, only created to add to his answer. His needs were so much greater than mine, but only by his greater than sign. Not really, just his algorithm which broke all natural rules or perhaps was formed by them. His road, the only road and mine the road not taken. Or rather, taken the ways that took him, took him away from me.

They may also be another, of course. If my screaming foetus is right. Another who can carry the blame.

Chapter Twelve

I walk as two men walking. Walking towards justice. Walking with a swagger. A belly swagger. Yet hands clenched. Fingers curling and uncurling over imaginary triggers. I cross the courtyard, the dust bowl, the empty centre space. The swing doors to the sheriff's office swing before me, swing open and then close with an ominous bang behind me.

Adrenaline is coursing through my body like a live current. I am a woman on a mission. I want to tell them what happened, why he died: the truth. I rap on the window frame, it opens, and the desk sergeant looks at me wearily over rimmed glasses. I start to tell him, but he stops me. Cuts me short. Wait, he says. Let me get the appropriate person to speak with you. Please take a chair and wait.

And so, I wait. And wait. I wait for four fucking hours for Superintendent Fucking Joe Dooley to get in. Waiting is what the British do. Patiently and in line. A nation of grocers. A nation of waiters. Haha, that is too funny. Waiting yes, waiters no. The English, in common with the Irish, have not a traditional excellence in restaurants. But we Irish do not do waiting. We have not that in common. I am so fucking hacked off. I cross every twenty minutes, every five minutes, to ask if Mr Prick Almighty is in.

I do not actually use those words you understand but my growing frustration is clear. It ripples in waves across the waiting area, one table, three chairs and a pile of poxy out of date magazines. I am tired of reading the posters on the walls. I am tired of this dusty God forsaken place. I am tired of watching people walk in, sort out their car tax issues, pay fines and get forms signed. Why do I have to wait for the prick?

The answer comes dropping slow. I am, after four excruciating hours, finally sitting in front of Superintendent Dooley. He listens; I tell. At length. He takes some notes. When I get to the point about the phone and not having it, he takes more notes. But that is it. I am not sure what I expected. I think perhaps a denouement of Sherlock Holmes proportions.

"That is very interesting," is all he says. And closing over his notebook. "Thank you for your time," and he rises from his chair. Force of habit makes me follow suit.

But now I am shouting. "Don't you see what this means?" I shout. "Don't you understand? Whoever had my phone, made that call. Lured him there. Pushed him over. Don't you fucking understand?"

Super Prick Intendent looks me in the eye. We are eyeball to eyeball, and I think I may have sprayed him a little with spittle. He blinks anyway with the force of the air leaving my lungs and the proximity of our faces. He is not a tall man and could rival my bump with his pot belly.

"Bella," he says calmly and with some resignation. "Where do you think you are? In a novel?"

"Of course I'm in a novel," I shout in reply. "Why else would I fucking curse so much and my dog have a leading speaking part. Just who is mad here?"

"Bella," he says calmly and with some resignation. "Your phone was found beside him. We discovered he sent several texts from your phone, some to his partner, some to his mother. His own phone was also there, but with no credit. I don't know why he texted himself, perhaps he had misplaced his phone, and wanted to find it. Why he had your phone, I don't know. But there was nothing sinister except for the poor man's brain which had cracked."

From the side, his brain had cracked. Out poured his sense and in flew a couple of blue birds with weeping eyes and tired feathers. They circled in the empty space and then nested on a tired tree, huddling together but they could find no warmth, no abiding place. They were not to stay and in a flash circled up again and this time flew straight out of the crack of his brain, leaving it totally bereft. In a panic, his sightless eyes watched them go and knew if he did not follow, he would never see them again.

He reached up and put out his arms and spinning, walking, falling, stepped out into the air. It was not enough to hold him of course. It's very thin, is air. Even when not in space. It's there but terribly unsubstantive. And Liam didn't have wings, didn't have a hovercraft waiting and while he may have lived in a novel, there was no deus ex machina to save him. Plop, went his shoe first, hit the half water, half bank. Followed very quickly by the rest of Liam and it wasn't a pretty sight. If a tree falls in the forest and no one hears it, does it still fall? And what happens to the noise? Does it circle the earth like a whisper, always travelling in time, never finding a home?

No one heard the loud thump the rest of Liam's body would have made, the crash and sickening crack of bones, the crush of flesh, the oily bubble of blood oozing from the now corpse onto the soil. There is still blood remaining on the bank. The boisterous show off boys from the village have seen it. They stuck their fingers in it, rubbed the stain off on their trousers. Then kicked the soil contemptuously. What did they fear of death? They were young and immortal unlike the sad fucker who dropped like a stone but who burst like an over ripe fruit.

Chapter Thirteen

The truth is very brittle in the morning. It shatters into a million pieces, and the picture painted the day before is gone in a second. All the thoughts, the theories, the conversations, the beliefs held so strongly are split into a million little shards and fall away, spiking the dust or falling into water, tumbling in the forest or just lying on the footpath. Each piece of truth finds its own level or homeplace, and there it stays put. It is now independent of its related truths and when they are not connected are they still a common truth or do they need connection for validity. Does the truth stand by itself, or does it fall connected?

I go to my mother to seek a truth. I can see she is not well. She is not that happy to see me. She extends a hand and almost brushes her fingers against my belly, but stops short. She is breathless.

"Did he?" I ask. She just looks at me. She says nothing for a while.

"You always wanted answers," she says at last. "And I rarely had any."

So, no change there then. My brain is swirling, and I genuinely don't know what to do. I am running out of road.

"What am I going to do, Mother?"

Chapter Fourteen

It all ended when the giant spaceship choose that very moment to park up in Ballybawn. Its spinning frame and piercing lights were bright even in daylight. The locals ran screaming from their houses, to their houses, from their houses, to their houses in tiny circles, in fear. Then the front portal opened and out came ET and told them he was home.

Of course, I am chosen to go back with them. For three months I sojourn with the aliens. They prod me a bit, look at my teeth, fit brain sensors onto my brain. They are very curious about my belly and spend hours looking at my unborn child who goos and coos at them through my tightly stretched skin. They are very impressed that I can create life. When I explain how it is done they laugh for three solid days. They only brought me back because they don't have any male specimens to check out my outlandish and wild claims. But they are still very impressed that I am growing a baby.

I ask if they can grow life too?. They shake their admittedly funny upside heads, and sadly say no. I am very upset. I had hoped with their superior intelligence they could have grown Liam again, from a cell or a drop of blood, ala Jurassic Park. I am dreadfully upset over this news. It doesn't seem fair but it turns out they are hermaphrodites and live for a long time. I haven't established how long, since their sense of time is different to mine. They also don't seem to form attachments as we do, nor dislikes. Which makes them a little cold. But they do like a good laugh. I only have to say sex and they fall about the place, holding their, admittedly inverted sides, and say oh dear, oh dear, oh dear.

I ask them about world peace, but since they do not fight, peace has no meaning for them. How weird I think. You definitely need a contrast to put the good things into sharp relief. If you don't fight, then you don't get to make up. And if you don't get to make up, then you never get to have make up sex. But shit, I forget, they don't do sex, period.

Actually, they are quite boring fuckers and once I get over the initial delight in making them laugh, I am bored shitless, witless, titless. Actually, that is a lie, I have never been more titful as my baby grows and my tits now need planning permission to enter a room.

I suppose though, it is good to relax. It is good to grow a baby. It is good to not think about Liam landing like a ripe fruit and splashing his body all over the ground. I especially like not thinking about Liam's body messed up on the ground. It's good not to have to think about that much.

It all ends when I am discharged. The aliens finally say that I am safe to return to earth. I am a bit disappointed as I wanted to learn some earth-shattering truths to share at home, literally. But they have taught me nothing. I have just been on a baby growing mission. That part has been very successful. I am ripe as a peach, not the peach that Liam was seconds before he fell, but an intact, living breathing entity.

Brigid is waiting for me as I disembark. She holds my hand. She has been to see me many times, she tells me, but I don't remember her on the spaceship. Just like I don't remember Liam's spilt body on the ground. It's very good not to remember.

What I don't remember mostly happened just before the spaceship landed in our sleepy village and drove the poor locals mad with fear. I only know because the aliens tell me some, and Brigid tells me some and even George tells me some.

Actually, it was George who spills the beans when I get home. He is so excited to see me, see the pendulous tits, the jam-packed belly, that he barks like a mad thing. "Take a life, give a life," he yelps. And he says this all day. I am tired and I ignore him at first. Finally, I give in and look at him, and he helps me remember.

What I don't remember happens like this. I am running out of road fast. I know how my phone ended up with Liam, and I know he didn't send those texts. I know my mother knows. I know, she knows and even Colin Powell fucking knows the things he knows. I watch and she gets up from the chair. I am surprised she has the strength. I don't say anything, I just watch. Then she goes to the cabinet and takes out a gun. Funny that, how a loaded gun can just be there, to hand, ready for any domestic, or intruder, any little plan for a murder you might have, or rather your mother might have. I know what mother plans, and I only watch. She calls Brent. The pub is practically empty. Afternoon service is very quiet and uneventful. Well, not this one, suckers.

He walks in. He has no fucking idea. He is all about the action, the deed done. He has no fucking clue. The surprise that spreads across his face is only matched by the red circle spreading across his chest. The retort fells mother, and she is lying in her chair, watching with clarity. Brent looks first at mother but then at me. His anger is all at me, but he is dead. Dead man walking. He does take a step but like a drunk man. He is gushing blood now. Did the bullet sever an artery? I remember now thinking about the volume of blood and how could there be so much?. Lady Macbeth had nothing on me. How long could he stand there and literally bleed. Suddenly, I hear a second shot, and I look at Brent trying to figure out where she has got the bastard this time. His knee caps perhaps, maybe an eye socket? I look but no more red appears, outside of course of the river of blood flowing from his chest. If I am perplexed, then so too is Brent, for he looks down at his bloody body with his eyebrows raised.

It is only when I look back at mother, at the shooter, do I realise where the second bullet has gone. She no longer has a face; it is torn away from the nose down. I am in a horror film. There is blood and guts and flesh at all sides of me. Brent is still swaying and looking as though he wants to walk towards me. Mother is pumping blood from what was her face. I guess the cancer is not going to kill her anymore. I look back at Brent and hope to fuck he is dead, or I am going to be very cross at mother, very cross indeed.

Finally, he himself tells me.

"I am dead" and falls. Thank the fuck. I look back at mother. "That was some answer mother," I say. "One fucking big answer I'd say."

And though she looks pretty ugly with half her face missing, she has never looked as beautiful to me as she did at that moment. And then the spaceship came and took me away.

Chapter Fifteen

Sweet Jesus. I am Mother. I look into the eyes of my mewling newborn, and I have only questions, no answers. And I am only beginning. We are only beginning. I have run out of my old road, and bang smack into a new one. Who knew new life took you back to the start again. I think I may have passed Go. I may have collected my child, but I don't want to stay playing my old game of monopoly. I want a fresh start. Please God let me not go back to my old road. Sweet Jesus let me find a new way. Two roads diverged in a yellow wood but which fucking road should I take now.

I am Mother.

A Thank You!

Thank you so much for joining us on Bella's journey in *Running Out of Road.*

At Whitney Morgan Media, we believe in the power of stories to uplift and connect us. Your voice as a reader is a vital part of that magic.

If Jillian Godsil's novel touched you, we'd be deeply grateful if you could take a moment to leave a review. Your feedback not only supports Jillian as an author but also helps fellow readers discover books that move, challenge, and inspire.

Every review—no matter how brief—makes a real difference. Thank you for supporting independent publishing and for helping us honor the stories that matter.

P.S. Love the book? Explore The Jillian Godsil Collection on Story. (storystore.io) for exclusive merch: mugs, journals, tote bags, and a few other items inspired by "George the Dog". It's one more way to keep the story close and share the journey.

With gratitude,
Rionna Morgan & The Whitney Morgan Media Team

www.ingramcontent.com/pod-product-compliance
Lightning Source LLC
Chambersburg PA
CBHW050926030726
47503CB00007BB/2489